I0669297

Glimpses of
God's Own Country

Striving to Write with Bite

Glimpses of
God's Own Country

Striving to Write with Bite

Editors
Francis Gonsalves
Ella Sonawane

2019

Glimpses of God's Own Country: Striving to Write with Bite- published by the Rev. Dr. Ashish Amos of the Indian Society for Promoting Christian Knowledge (ISPCK), Post Box 1585, Kashmere Gate, Delhi-110006 under Women's Empowerment Programme Series (WEP-43).

© Editors, 2019

All rights reserved. No part of this book may be reproduced or transmitted in any form or by any means, electronic, mechanical, photocopying, recording, or by any information storage and retrieval system, without the prior permission in writing from the publisher.

The views expressed in the book are those of the contributors and the publisher takes no responsibility for any of the statements.

Online order: http://ispck.org.in/book.php

Also available on amazon.in

ISBN: 978-93-88945-08-0

Laser typeset by

ISPCK, Post Box 1585, 1654, Madarsa Road, Kashmere Gate, Delhi-110006 • *Tel:* 23866323

e-mail: ashish@ispck.org.in • ella@ispck.org.in
website: www.ispck.org.in

Contents

Preface

For fruitfully reflecting upon crucial concerns that affect us all, what better place to choose than 'God's Own Country': Kerala? For seeking clarity on these same concerns, which better spot in Kerala to plant oneself than beside the rapid and restless Periyar River? For getting gutsy, yet godly, insights into current crises that confront us, which better group to tap than twenty-plus millennials, bubbling with ideals and overflowing with insights like the Periyar in spate? '*Glimpses of God's Own Country: Striving to Write with Bite*' throws open windows to gaze upon life in all its beauty and complexity. It offers you fledgling writings of a group of youth committed to life and concerned about church, country and cosmos.

This book is the fruit of a writers' workshop organized by ISPCK—Indian Society for Promotion of Christian Knowledge—a premier publishing house for more than three hundred years, in collaboration with the Jesuit-run LIPI—Loyola Institute of Peace and International Relations—Kochi, Kerala. ISPCK aims at promoting the Good News of Jesus Christ through the effective use of the media.

Besides having hundreds of eminent authors, worldwide, publishing their works with the ISPCK, it also aims at tapping new talent for budding writers to 'write with bite' so as to catalyze conversations in church and society about issues of importance.

The essays in this book were written in the short span of three days, when a group of twenty-five handpicked youth assembled at the scenic *Sameeksha* Meditation Centre, Kalady, situated on the banks of the Periyar. Among those enrolled at the writers' workshop were young university professors and professionals, youth from various colleges and committed grassroot activists, as well as a couple of religious brothers and nuns. All came for one purpose: to put on their thinking caps, to put pen to paper, and to voice their views in public though eventual publication. Providing inputs to hone writing and editorial skills, were the resource persons: Rev. Dr. Ashish Amos, General Secretary and Director, ISPCK; Ms. Ella Sonawane, Assistant General Secretary,Publishing & Mission, ISPCK; Dr. Binoy Pichalakkattu and Dr. Roy Thottam LIPI, and Prof. Francis Gonsalves, *Jnana-Deepa Vidyapeeth*, Pune.

Flipping through the pages of this book you will read interesting and insightful articles on a wide array of topics in diverse domains: (a) theological – on who Jesus really is; (b) spiritual – stressing the values of silence, tolerance and faith; (c) social – discussing the problem of drugs, gender inequality and cultural stereotyping, as well as the pathetic plight of migrant workers, marginalized women and transgenders; (d) political – on the threats of stifling democratic dissent and peddling lies in politicking; (e) health – exploring the healing touch and coping with disabilities; (f) family life – about parenting and child abuse; (g) education – assessing our learning system and critiquing discrimination in the education of women; (h) ecology – suggesting how to care for mother earth and conserve her energy, and, (h) communications – exposing the dangers of social media trolls and the deluge of emojis in SMSs.

Kerala has the commendable distinction of being *numero uno* among Indian states in terms of having the highest literacy rate, as well as highest gender ratio of 1084 females to 1000 males. That healthy gender ratio was seen in the composition of the writers, as there were more young women than men! Understandably, in this collection, there are articles which critique our heavily patriarchal society, which frequently forces women to settle for subordinate roles in church and society. But the participants were determined to call a spade a spade and to make their voices heard. That they did—including a nun who extolled woman power and stressed that a nun is second to none. Although most of the articles have a serious tone, there's also a dash of humour on some pages as someone confessed her dread of dogs tailing her. She scripted her 'bytes on bites'!

Much water has flowed down the Periyar from the time of the Writers' Workshop till this publication sees the light of day. Sadly, in the interim period, Kerala suffered its worst ever flood in a century. Were this workshop to be conducted thereafter, we would certainly have articles on the same, including scribblings on more current issues like the Sabarimala Temple stalemate. The resource persons hope that these, and other issues of public pertinence, will be addressed in due time by the very same group of brave, budding authors.

ISPCK seeks to make Jesus' Good News reach the ends of the earth. LIPI desires that all of us be channels of God's peace. Best-selling spiritual author, Prof. Sebastian Painadath— Director of *Sameeksha*—always strives to harmonize the human, divine and cosmic. May the experiences of being together in God's Own Country and strivings to write with bite, continue to reap rich harvests so that the Good News of Christ may reach every person and every place, for everyone to become channels of God's peace.

The Editors

Silenced Silence
Ajith Chittilappilly

Last month one of my cousins told me, "I saw a movie yesterday. It was rather slow and background music was lacking most of the time. I felt it to be quite boring." I also watched the same movie after a few days. The makers of that film had made use of silence to a great extent. In fact that movie is rich in content and it conveys a good message. Yet, my cousin felt it to be quite boring. This is the mental frame of the postmodern generation.

People of the contemporary world are so busy with their hectic schedules that they even forget about their own health, both physical as well as mental. The changing trends of society have changed the lifestyle of people. Where is our society going? What is our generation running after? After all, everybody comes to a conclusion that life is meaningless. No one has time to sit down and listen to their inner breaths in silence. In this noisy world, the role of silence itself has got silenced, i.e., silence has been silenced.

It is time to encourage our youngsters and the middle aged to slow down and enter into an interior world of silence. It is necessary to build up an inner temple of silence from where we can draw a great deal of peace and tranquillity throughout our life.

Similar is the case of the Christian world. Christianity is day by day lacking the sense of interior spirituality. We are busy with many liturgical ceremonies and ritualistic activities. Often we neglect the role of silent meditations. Retreat centres with massive loudspeakers are on the increase. Pastors who follow the path of serenity and calmness are very few, and also not in demand. So, a new turn is needed in the Christian sphere too.

Silence literally means complete lack of noise or sound. Broadly we can divide it into three levels: physical, psychic and spiritual. Physical silence means not only keeping our lips closed in order not to communicate anything with others but also to attain a relaxed state of bodily stillness. Here our aim is to shut out all extraneous noises and movements.

The second level is the psychic's level of silence. Here we move on to the particular elements that make up our psyche or the mind. These involve the faculties of imagination, emotions, memory, intellect and will. At this level we seek to silence all these mental faculties in order to bring our spirit into a deeper oneness and awareness. The third and the deepest level of silence is spiritual silence. From the mind we are going deep into the level of the soul. All thoughts and reflections are silenced. Here our soul encounters the ultimate being – God. In this complete silence our souls become empty receptacles to receive

Ajith Chittilappilly

the Spirit's gifts of faith, hope and love. Only at this level can we readily hear the inner voice of God's Spirit.

This pure inner silence has many characteristics. First of all it is an act of undoing. It is not of doing or thinking anything forcefully. It is simply the process of undoing, which happens spontaneously. Of course, we need a deliberate effort to go through the levels of physical and mental silences. But in the case of the innermost level, our efforts will not do. It naturally flows. The only thing we can do is to desire it earnestly and make that desire a prayer.

Another feature of silence is that it involves listening. In the book of Psalms we read – "Be still, and know that I am God" (Ps 46:10). Listening involves opening up of our own mind and spirit to the words and the actions of God. In other words, it is the inner attentiveness to the divine interventions. Here silence becomes the milieu in which the voice of God is being heard and we surrender our will to God's Spirit.

Silence harmonises our body, mind, and spirit. This sense of harmony and unity is yet another feature of silence. It tunes the whole person in such a way that one acts out from inner convictions and motivations. One who enjoys the sweetness of internal silence will be very well balanced in one's daily affairs. Various compartments of that person – body, mind, spirit – will be in a perfect alignment.

Silence enables one to open up one's mind to receive and hear others. The person becomes broadminded. Since one gains the skill of listening one can accommodate any kind of people in the friendship circle. Consequently, one begins to respect and accept the different opinions and attitudes of others.

Silence is a process of self-emptying too. When we pass through the different levels of silence we empty various elements of our being such as thinking, imagining, dreaming and intellect. This kinetic experience makes our social sensitivity to transcendental realities.

Let's think about the necessity of silence in the contemporary world. It is the urgent need of the time to enliven the silenced silence. The modern generation knows everything about the spiritual world within. On the one hand, the youth nowadays spend time in thrills, shocks, and fantasy; and, on the other hand, they lose the real thrills of the true spirit.

Science and philosophy from the various corners of the world are in competition to gain the market. New ideas and intellectual reflections are getting accumulated day by day in the public forum. But we have no time to silently reflect upon any idea and internalize the main contents. Without assimilation the ideologies simply pass by. Thinkers would say that the unreflected ideas are sheer waste. In that sense, our intellectual and moral circles have become a huge waste basket.

A sense of inner silence and peace of mind will solve a whole lot of problems and conflicting issues that cause disturbances at the local, national and international levels. Our gentle silence is enough in many situations to prevent the outbreak of unnecessary and unhealthy disputes and quarrels. A wise rethinking or recollection in silence may reduce our stubbornness and help us change our attitudes and decisions. This will foster the interpersonal relations and comradeship among persons and communities.

Identity crisis is an alarming problem that is curbing the vitality of energetic youth in this era. Self knowledge is often said to be the greatest of all knowledge. This self knowledge is not at all inborn. It is gained or acquired through personal discoveries, mainly by sincere introspection. Silence plays an important role in effective introspection. Without a silent mind and heart we cannot know the very core of our being. By attaining genuine self knowledge and self awareness the problem of identity crisis can be solved to a great extent.

The modern generation hates loneliness or solitude. Youngsters are engaged in whiling their evenings away with their friends either in the physical world or in the digital world. Anyhow, they dislike seclusion. As a result they cannot face challenges alone. The rate of suicide is alarmingly increasing. They deliberately silence the role of silence in their lives. In short, they lack maturity at the mental and spiritual levels. Practice of effective silent episodes in daily life can provide them with adequate will power and deep maturity level.

Silence does not mean being silent in every walk of life. But it means a matured way of looking at and responding to reality. Silence is not something unproductive. In fact it is highly productive. It produces the fruits of wisdom, charity and prudence. It is not something inactive or dull. But it is highly active and vibrant in the inner spirit. Silence is not something wholly dedicated to monks and contemplatives. It is very much needed and useful to every human being, especially to all of us in this fast moving generation.

The teaching of the Holy Bible to go to the inner silent space and meet the Divine therein can be taken as a good conclusion. "When you pray, go into your inner room, close the door and pray to the Father who is in the secret space" (Mt 6:6). It makes clear that silence is a spiritual space of vital importance where we encounter the ultimate in simplicity and purity. This mystical power of silence is to be brought into awareness of the current hi-fi and wi-fi generation. Let's break the silence of silence and engage in the world with this renewed "mystic consciousness" to render a new quality life.[2]

Endnotes

[1] George A. Maloney, *The Silence of Surrounding Love: Body, Soul, Spirit Integration*, Bombay, St. Paul, 1991, 180.

[2] Sebastian Painadath, *The Power of Silence: Fifty Meditations to Discover the Divine Space Within You*, Delhi: ISPCK, 2011, 110.

Ajith Chittilappilly

The Disabled 'Us'

Aloysius T. Antony

A re you disabled? No? Then, this wave is going to capsize your boat.

What comes to your mind when you think of disability or disabled? Let me guess. May be pictures of people on crutches or wheelchairs or may be people with a walking stick and black goggles. Stephen Hawking or Helen Keller may come to mind or perhaps movies like 'Black' or 'Iqbal' may fill our mind. Probably belonging to the 21st century, you may also touch the realms of the evolving concept of 'technologically disabled'. But is that it?

Disability refers to a lack or shortage of something which limits our ability to something and generally we link it to the limitations we see externally. Thus the formula disability = blind or deaf or mute or crippled and so on. If so, then why is this article for you? You are not blind, or deaf. I want to invite you to delve a little deeper into the word 'disabled'. Does the word presuppose exteriority? Does it really limit itself to physical limitations? Perhaps, getting confined to external appearances is the product of the society we live in. Having said so, what does disability really mean?

I have been in touch with the so-called disabled people for the past couple of years. I learned the alphabet in sign language probably when I was in class 8. And they have been the happiest people I have ever seen. What makes them so happy despite their limitations and weaknesses? Despite their incapabilities, how is it that they are so satisfied? Have we ever imagined the dialogue they go through within themselves? "How does the world around me look like? I wish I could see", "Why are they clapping? Did she sing so well? I wish I could hear", "Rohit runs so fast. I wish I could run too." Their lives are full of many "I wish" but still they seem so satisfied, happy and alive. How do they do it? Generally, food, water and shelter are considered to be the basic necessities of life; but I guess vision, speech and strength would be for them. Therefore, despite lacking so much in life how do they dare even to smile? What is their magic mantra? For me, I guess it's 'acceptance'. They accept themselves as they are; therein lies the beauty of their life. Once considered as a curse, and even today, in some parts, the disabled welcome their weakness, short comings and limitations and move on with their lives. For me, it is here that their strength lies. They walk, they fall, but get up and move on. They try to visualise the dark world and find the correct path. They focus on the lip movement and try to get hold of the meaning. They'll do anything but will never stop.

You and I are, by contrast, the so-called 'normal' people. Physically almost fine; able and capable. However, not among

Aloysius T. Antony

the happiest or satisfied people. Here lies the irony. Despite having everything right externally, we lack something and thus feel unsatisfied. Why? I guess we, the normal, able and capable, find it hard accepting ourselves as we are – our weaknesses and shortcomings – we forget about overcoming them. As our limitations are not something exterior or visible we try our best to hide them with covers and coats of superficiality. We become so obsessed with "what will others think?" that we never visualise a correct path, find it difficult to rise after a fall, and thus, are easily stoppable. From our dress, style, way of walking and talking to the subjects we choose to pursue, to the movies we watch, to the people we choose to hang out with, everything has a pinch of 'the other' – what will others think. I am not saying we must live in isolation with the notion of 'the other' but it should not influence us so much that we lose our true selves. The disabled cannot hear or see others, they don't bother so much about 'what others think'. But just imagine as soon as one realises the 'who' and 'how' and starts thinking about what others would think one wouldn't dare to do the very same thing one loved. These complexes creep into our lives and we start identifying with other people. In our effort to be in the 'mainstream' add many superficial make ups forgetting and hiding our real self, our nature and talents.

I had a friend who loved *Bharatnatyam*, learned it for 6 years but still hesitated to perform in public because the people he was surrounded with linked classical dances to something feminine. Another one, who generally loves to help others, stepped back to help certain 'unpopular' people despite the fact that he genuinely wanted to help them. So you see, how we damage ourselves by letting 'the other' influence us. And I guess that's where we need to stop a while and think 'why'. Why do we let others influence us so much that we give up on the very things we cherish? The disabled on the other hand know what they are, their strengths and their weaknesses and thus focus on their strength and blossom from disabled to differently abled.

By focussing on their strength they turn even their minuses into plus. Our problem is we neither have a clear idea about our strong points, nor our weak points, and so dwindle between the two somehow managing to fit in the 'normal' or accepted category. We long so much to be accepted by others that we forget to accept ourselves. If we don't approve ourselves of what we like, how can we focus on improving ourselves? Here, I would like to take you back to what disability means. It refers to something which limits our ability to do something. Now, I leave it to you to decide who the real disabled are. Those who are externally disabled or those who are internally disabled? Those who accept themselves as they are and try to bloom where they are planted, in the way they are planted or those who, instead of accepting themselves, seek acceptance and approval from the society or other people?

One thing we all must understand is that we all have infirmities and weaknesses and it is the combination of our capacities and infirmities that makes us unique and special and this uniqueness we must cherish.

Aloysius T. Antony

Dangers of Drugs

Amal Tom George

Kerala is the land of '*kera*' – coconut trees. It is called '*kalpavriksha*' as every part of the tree is useful in one way or the other. But we are now concerned about a plant which is harmful and useless to common people. In Kerala, substance abuse among teenagers (high school students) is increasing in an alarming rate, where the widespread contraband is cannabis.

Substance abuse is the act of using psychoactive substances and illicit drugs including alcohol in a harmful, hazardous manner. Kerala tops the chart of alcohol use in the country with 20-30% prevalence of alcoholism. The shocking factor is that the age of first drinking has decreased from 19 years to 13 years. But there is a change in the trend of substance abuse. Today, teenagers bypass alcohol use and take recourse in drug abuse, which is more harmful and rehabilitation nearly impossible.

Activity of drug mafia in the state is increasing day by day. From cultivation of drugs to transhipment and hijacking enforcement to market research, diverse activities are being intensified. The Narcotic Control Bureau (hereafter abbreviated as NCB), which is an apex agency, warns about the latest marketing strategy of the drug mafia. The NCB says that the drug mafia constructs a consumer network using teenagers. Teenagers are exploited by taking advantage of their peer pressure. Once anyone reaches to a substance abuser level one can easily be used to canvas among one's peer group.

The next stage of a substance abuser is a street peddler. Drug suppliers gives dealership to abusers. The substance abuser-teenager finds the income generated through peddling as a potential source for his/her daily need of drugs. This peddling is a part time activity. But gradually the priorities of the teenager change and they start drug selling as a full time activity. This leads them to severe criminal activities. Police hesitate to fix charges and register cases on minors because of two reasons. One of the reasons is that the drug substance will be of very minimal quantity, which is not sufficient to register a case; and the other reason is the concern about the future of that teenager.

School students are not checked by police officers because they trust them as we normally do. Moreover, school uniforms are a dress code having privileges in any public transport system. These two factors are misused. It is alarming to note that the NCB arrested a drug dealer from Vayander who used school students for carrying drugs across borders. Law and order personnel find it very difficult to curb this menace without the help and support of parents. Many parents deny the findings of police, defend their children and give excuses for their children's behaviour. And when the parents realise the truth it will be very late to do something.

The population of Kerala can be divided into three class-segments: elite class, middle class and lower class. The major chunk of the population is middle class. Moral values and social restrictions make this class less exposed to such illicit activities. By contrast, when we consider both the upper class and the lower class, we find that the number of drug abusers is high in both classes. Peer pressure is a key player in this game. In the lower class teenagers finds it very important to be a part of a group. In this case peer pressure becomes the problem of their identity and existence.

Members of the elite class are lonely. Having enough time and resources they search for new pleasures and finally end up in drugs. This is the general picture of people who get into such activities.

What happens to high school students after taking drugs? The answer is simple. Consider a chemical laboratory where numerous chemical reactions take place. All reactions are controlled and supervised. When a teenager abuses a drug, it is like carrying out an unwanted, uncontrolled chemical reaction in his/her brain. Teenage (from 13 to 19 years) is the time when crucial development of brains takes place.

Chemical substances which have well defined uses when abused for psychoactive purposes create adverse effect on the neural system. A reprogramming of one's brain takes place. This change is plastic, which means nearly irreversible. Thus, the priority of an individual is hijacked. Drugs take the position of food and water in the priority list of the brain. Then they start thinking that drugs are the elements which sustain their life. This reprogramming of brain makes rehabilitation difficult.

How does a teenager end up using drugs? There are a number of reasons why a teenager starts using drugs. Among these, there is a reason which can be avoided if we change our attitude towards teenagers. Restrictions and judgements are showered upon them from home, school and society. We forget to respect their space and privacy. They are often under the cloud of suspicion. Enormous pressure is applied by their being subject to tight academic schedules. All natural outlets for entertainment and fun are forbidden to teenagers due to these factors. Our attitude, which is not at all friendly towards teenagers, is a major reason to turn a teenager into a drug addict.

Let us consider a situation when a teenager student is caught for possession of drugs. He/she will be branded as a chronic drug addict. This stigma and shame do more harm than drugs. Police officers are often kind in dealing with such cases; but society is not. What can a teenager do to overcome his addiction without the support of society? One is helpless.

There is a misconception that a drug abuser can be identified from his/her external appearances. This is a himalayan blunder. Some drugs are difficult to detect in blood tests. How can someone identify a substance abuser who uses inhalants by testing blood? Serious behavioural change is the only visible symptom of drug abuse and this is shown at a critical stage of drug abuse.

So how can we identify and detect presence of drugs in the life of a teenager. Just get into his/her shoes. Try to know their friends. Find time to talk with them. Above all, express the love which we keep hiding. As peer pressure is the only channel through which drugs reach to a teenager, make a filter

Amal Tom George

to segregate the friend circle of a teenager. Dear parents, please welcome the friends of your children to your home. This is the only way you can get in touch with their activity circle. This is the only possibility to keep children away from hidden friends.

What are the social hazards of drug abuse among teenagers? This is a question which is not asked because our society has not yet answered the question about social hazards of drug abuse among adults. Teenage is the period of life which makes individuals pay with their life for the convictions they have. If we who care for teenagers fail to convince them that we love and value them and will always be there for them, the drug mafia takes over this function of ours to further foster their agenda.

It is our duty to become aware of the situation. Act according to the needs and support anti drug awareness activities. It is very important to maintain our presence of mind when we are exposed to drug abuse cases in our proximity. If you find your child, student, friend is a drug abuser, reach out to the nearest helping hand.

The NCB's always available helpline (number 9495823751 in Kerala) keeps your identity safe if you inform them about drug dealing activities. There are many effectively functioning non-profit organisations who are 24×7 available to give guidance in dealing with a substance abuser. They conduct awareness programs, one to one reach out programs, rehabilitation, free psychological support and counselling.

It is our duty to act wisely to save our vibrant generation from the greedy teeth and filthy hands of the drug mafia.

Protect Mother Earth:
A Christian Response

Amardeep, SJ

Two months ago, I stayed three days at Sahajeevana Kendram, Kannur—an initiative of the Kerala Jesuit Society to promote ecological awareness among people, especially among children and youth. What makes this place so special is that the house (*ettukettu*) is in the midst of a wide variety of plants and trees. At Sahajeevana Kendram, the use of any plastic items, synthetic food, and cosmetic items like soaps, perfumes, detergents, etc., is strictly prohibited. People have meals from one plate with two or three persons sharing a plate. This haven fills one with so much energy and hope that one never feels like returning home from there. I certainly did not feel like leaving. My sentiments were shared by the couple of hundred students who visited 'Sahajeevana Kendram' in the span of those three days. Here is a real-existing place where human beings live in harmony with one another and with mother nature. A replica of the Garden of Eden, indeed!

Now let's look at another image, a sharply contrasting one. Last year, I was in a South Indian city for a few months. Across the road where I lived there was a housing society with many huge flats. The buildings and the premises were a concrete jungle; there was hardly any soil to be seen. The place was devoid of plants and trees, too. What caught my attention was the lives of children living in that building. Every morning some school buses would come to pick them up and in the afternoon the buses would drop them back. The kids were never seen playing outdoor games at all. They had hardly any interaction with other human beings; and no contact whatsoever with mother nature.

I think that most of us can identify our situation with the second image. These days it is neither uncommon to see one wearing a mask on the streets in order to protect oneself from air pollution, nor is it rare to spot one frightened to get into even the apparently cleanest water bodies to avoid contracting waterborne diseases caused by pollution. That we live in a polluted world is an undeniable fact.

Everyday, thousands and thousands of people lose their lives due to some direct or indirect effects of various kinds of pollution. The number of people suffering from respiratory disorders, skin cancers and so on is increasing on a daily basis. The pollution produced by us human beings by the use of insecticides, pesticides, fertilizers, burning of fossil fuels, etc., badly affect not just us, human beings, but the whole of creation too. The sad thing is that though all of us know that these things are taking place worldwide we tend to do absolutely nothing about it. This silence and indifference of the people who know about these crucial issues, the proper addressal of which is of utmost importance for the well being of the earth, is frightening.

Unless every human being takes a firm decision that he/she would never do anything that would harm his/her fellow beings and the whole creation, no substantial change can take place. What prevents most of us from taking such steps is our own selfishness. This selfishness gives rise to greed. The uncontrollable greed of even a single person can have a tremendously bad impact on the environment. The saddest thing is that it is not the greedy and the rich who suffer most of the dire consequences of their own greed-ridden actions but the poor and the marginalised.

Though pollution affects everything on this planet, it has a more severe impact on the poor. For instance, tanning is an industrial activity that results in a lot of pollution. Most of the labourers in the tanning industry suffer from various diseases, and as a result, their lifespan is severely reduced. By contrast, most of the owners of this industry enjoy good health because they never come in direct contact with pollutants. Also, since they are rich they can afford to have air purification and similar devices in their houses. This is certainly a form of injustice. Jesuit Samuel Rayan rightly points out in his article 'Theology of Justice in Relation to Ecology': "When wealth and the earth resources are diverted from serving the community's needs and possibilities and are withdrawn from common control, people become socially marginalised, left without adequate means of life and dignity."

Now the big question is: what can we really do to protect the earth from going through an ecological catastrophe? When

I think about it two images come to my mind. The first one is that of St. Francis of Assissi and the second one is that of an ancient Indian sage.

In his encyclical letter '*Laudato Si*', Latin, meaning, 'Praise be to You', Pope Francis says the following about St. Francis: "I believe that St. Francis is the example par excellence of care for the vulnerable and of an integral ecology lived out joyfully and authentically... He communed with all creation, even preaching to the flowers, inviting them to 'praise the Lord', just as if they were endowed with reason." St Francis indeed was a mystic who was able to find 'God in all things'. In his novel 'God's Pauper', which is based on the life of St. Francis, Nikos Kazantskis, the well known Greek writer, describes such a scene. When Francis sees a bird looking up at the sky after drinking some water, he tells his companion Br. Leo: "Look Leo, that bird is thanking God by lifting its head towards the sky." How wonderful the world would have been if only we had imbibed the spirit of St. Francis! How peaceful the world would have been if we could also look at our fellow human beings and the rest of creation and could address them as 'sisters and brothers' like St. Francis did.

The second image is that of an ancient Indian sage who is about to take his first step of the day in the morning on the earth. Hundreds of years ago, our ancestors used to recite the following Sanskrit prayer before they first put their feet on the ground:

Samudra vasane devi
Parvatha sthana mandale

Vishnu pathni namasthu bhyam
Pada sparsa shamasya me

This can loosely be translated as: "O goddess earth, the wife of Vishnu, whose attire is the oceans and body the mountains, pardon me for I am about to keep my feet on you." It is difficult to find prayers that express such great reverence towards the earth like the one mentioned above. And it is a matter of great shame that we Indians who used to revere the earth as a goddess have come down to a state so low that we do not feel even a tinge of guilt for dumping tons of garbage on the earth. There are other ancient Indian prayers too that remind us of the importance to look at the whole of creation as manifestation of the divine itself. The verse '*Isavasyam idam sarvam*' (The whole universe is pervaded by the Lord) is one such prayer. Only when we are firmly convinced that the whole creation is the body of God and that hurting even the tiniest of creatures will cause pain to God, the divine itself, then will we cease to exploit, plunder and abuse the earth.

It is not enough that we live on with these convictions. We should take some practical steps as well. I think the following questions will help us all to come up with some practical solutions that would help us to foster and nurture ecology.

- Why can't we have our churches and religious houses in the model of Shajeevana Keendram that I mentioned before?

- Why can't we have more talks, seminars and prayer sessions based on the topic 'eco-spirituality' organised at various levels like parish, diocese, and national, and so on?

Amardeep, SJ

- There are thousands of Christian educational institutions all over the world. Why not the management in these institutions make it a point to have at least an hour a week for classes on environment and another hour for cleaning the campus and the premises, and once a month to organise 'ecological awareness' campaigns animated by students themselves?

- Why can't each diocese maintain an eco reserve on its own where most rare species of the flora and fauna of that locality are preserved?

- Why can't more Christians, especially the religious, work with organizations involved in the conservation of nature such as WWF, Greenpeace and so on?

- Why don't we start more publications which are secular in their outlook but at the same time are more focussed on ecology and related issues and eco literature?

- Why don't we Christians more often use public transport, electric vehicles and bicycles which are more eco-friendly rather than private vehicles which run on fossil fuels? Certainly such a step would involve some suffering. However it is good to keep in mind that in the long run the suffering will bear fruit.

- Why can't the church invest more on scientific researches which are on their way to invent cleaner and cheaper forms of energy, eco friendly technical appliances, etc.?

We shouldn't let these questions stay as mere questions, but we should take necessary steps at the earliest to put these into practice after necessary discussion and deliberations. Let us keep in mind the fact that the earth is the only home that we have. So, let all our actions be in favour of the promotion of life on our planet.

Amardeep, SJ

Hope amidst Hopelessness: Exploring Doubly Marginalised Afro African Women with Reference to Alice Walker

Angela Jinny

"Call them from their houses,
And teach them to dream"
- Jean Toomer

Amid the harsh restraints of slavery, Afro-American writers, especially black women in their endangerment, tried to preserve the culture of their ancestry and articulated their struggles, longings and dreams in their own words and images. A growing number of black female artists and writers emerged throughout the Civil War and Reconstruction eras. Toni Morrison was awarded the Nobel Prize for literature in 1993 for her body of work. She was the first African-American author to win the prestigious honour.

Black women want themselves to be a part of literature. They are proving the fact that they are not an inferior gender and passive objects. Women don't want to deny their dignity and worse, their identity. They are struggling for their basic rights. Some of the major black women writers are Maya Angelou, Harriet Jacobs, Maria Stewart, Toni Morrison, Alice Walker and Zora Neala Hurston. These black women writers want to regain their dignity, self esteem, self-realisation, and save their sexual awareness. Alice Walker's intention not only gives voice to black women but also provides for their freedom.

Afro-American or black women are treated as animals, losing their human rights and suffering inequality in society from Afro-American men. They want to break the fetters of patriarchy. They want to stop domestic violence perpetuated by Afro-American men. Afro-American men inflict heavy responsibility on their women to maintain the household by doing works such as cooking, cleaning and washing clothes.

Afro-American women want to break the power of patriarchy. They want to establish women empowerment against men. These women try to identify themselves and want to play the role of males. African American women are not only physically and economically assaulted by the white society, but also by the men of their own race.

The black woman had no protector and was used, and is still being used in some cases, as the scapegoat for the evils perpetrated by black men in this horrendous system. Moreover, her physical image has been maliciously maligned; she has been sexually molested and abused by the white coloniser. She has suffered the worst kind of economic exploitation. They have

Angela Jinny

been forced to serve as the white woman's maid and also for nursing white children while her own children were starving and neglected. African American women are facing not only poverty but also heavy burdens of labour.

Alice Walker's women characters display strength, endurance, and resourcefulness in confronting and overcoming oppression in their lives. Walker is depicting the devastating circumstances of the twin afflictions of racism and sexism. Walker writes through her feelings and her concepts of morals she has grown up with. She writes about the black women's struggle for spiritual wholeness and sexual, political and social equality. Walker's central characters are almost always black women and the themes of sexism and racism are predominant in her works. However, her impact is felt across both racial and sexual boundaries.

Alice Walker is a poet, novelist, short story writer, critic, essayist, and apologist for black women. The special identifying mark of her writing is her concern for the lives of black women. Her main preoccupation has been the souls of black women. Walker is committed to exploring the oppression, the insanities, the loyalties and the triumphs of black women. Walker has examined the external realities facing their women as well as the internal world of each woman.

Much of the narrative in Walker's novel is derived from her own personal experience, growing up as an uneducated and abused child. Walker describes the way that southern race relations, particularly the prevailing system of sharecropping, produced a painfully contradictory relationship between African Americans and the surrounding natural world. All her writing is aimed at inspiring and motivating black women to stand up for their rights.

Walker is an apologist and spokeswoman for black women. Her sense of personal identification with black women includes a sense of sharing in their peculiar oppression. At some length she describes her own attempts at suicide when she discovered herself pregnant in her last year of college and at the mercy of everything, especially her own body. Walker spoke of her own awareness and experiences with brutality and violence in the lives of black women, many of whom she had known as a girl growing up in Eatonton, Georgia, some in her own family. The recurrent theme running throughout much of her work of art is about women in her belief that black women are the most oppressed people in the world.

Walker believes that only a the black woman can speak for herself and tell her own story. Nineteenth century black foremothers were such women. Being doubly marginalised as both black and female, black women not only question mainstream society, but they also challenge other minority groups like Afro-Americans, on the one hand, and the feminists, on the other, as well. The term 'womanist' was first coined by Walker.

In Alice Walker's celebrated essay "In Search of our Mother's Garden's", she talks about the uncelebrated women of Afro-American origin. Walker's construction of womanism and the different meanings she invests in it is an attempt to situate the black woman in history and culture and at the same time rescue her from the negative and inaccurate stereotypes that mask her in African American society. First, Walker inscribes

Angela Jinny

the black woman as a knowing and thinking subject who is always in pursuit of knowledge, wanting to know more and in greater depth than is considered good for one, thus interrogating the epistemological exclusions she endures in intellectual life in general and feminist scholarship in particular. Second, she highlights black woman's agency, strength, capability and independence.

In "The Color Purple", Walker introduces Southern black female characters who not only faced slavery, but also sexism, racism and oppression. "The Color Purple" is an extraordinary account of a black woman's plight as she strives towards acceptance, freedom and independence. Like many other novels by Walker that are devoted to the mistreatment of black women, in this novel too she motivates black women to stand up for their rights.

It is idle dreaming to think of black women simply caring for their homes and children like the middle class white model. Most black women have to work to help house, feed, and clothe their families. Those who are exerting their manhood by telling black women to step back into a domestic, submissive role are assuming a counter revolutionary position. It is the time for everyone to erase the gender discrimination and to work cooperatively for the upliftment of the family and the society.

Throughout Walker's work the preservation of black culture prevails as important and her female characters forge important links to maintain continuity in both personal relationships and communities. The female, according to southern norms, should present herself as an epitome of passivity, chastity and demure beauty and should receive from men the rewards of security, comfort and respect.

So many black women have been crushed and utterly destroyed precisely because they are black and because they are women. Walker's works speak strongly of the experiences of black women. Critics have commented that the messages of her books transcend both race and gender. Women of a darker skin colour have a double experience of marginalisation on account of race and gender; they live and work with westerners. Racism and capitalism have trampled the potential of black people and thwarted their self determination.

During the last four decades remarkable transformations have taken place in Afro-American literature. Once dismissed as 'provincial' by white critics, the fictions of the Afro-American authors in the 1980s frequently appear on best sellers list. The most significant of all is that many of the pre-eminent leaders of this pioneering new fiction are black women, who were the invisible authors in a literary tradition. Their works are highlighting the sense of hope and aspiration or dream as a silver lining in the dark cloud of the black women's life for a bright and a happy future.

Angela Jinny

Impact of Media
in the Present Scenario
Anju Rose, SABS

"No man is an island," said the sixteenth century poet, John Donne. By their very essence, humans have been created as social creatures. Our daily lives are strongly affected by communication with others as well as by messages we receive from distant and unknown persons. The ability to communicate at a higher level separates human beings from other animals.

Communication is the exchange of ideas and feelings among people. Communication has the ability to multiply contacts within society, to deepen social consciousness and to bind individuals more closely to their fellow brothers and sisters. This process that will foster communication among human beings will serve to build new relationships and to fashion a new language which permits people to know themselves better and to understand one another more easily.

Communication revolution has had a profound impact on our world. Information and communication technology has changed rapidly over the past twenty years, with a key development being the emergence of social media.

The pace of change in communications is accelerating. Contemporary media offers marvellous new opportunities for us. For example, the development of mobile technology has played an important role in shaping the impact of social media. Communication media is relevant at every level of life. Across the globe, mobile devices dominate in terms of total minutes spent online.

Positive impact of media on society

We are living in a digital era. Media and its influence are growing day by day. People are so occupied with the use of various media such as internet, smart phones, Twitter, Facebook, WhatsApp, TV, etc. Social media is being used in ways that shape politics, business, world culture, education, careers, innovations and more.

The impact of social media on our society is growing fast. It helps us to create good connection with extended family and friends. It helps to develop better perspectives of various issues, learn new things, extend ideas and help hone networking skills. It also helps to provide an effective classroom for enhancing students' knowledge.

Almost a quarter of the world's population is now on Facebook. It shrinks the entire world into a global village. Without social media, social, ethical, environmental and political ills have minimal visibility. Increased visibility of issues has shifted the balance of power from the hands of a few to the masses.

Anju Rose, SABS

Social media also facilitates the development of technical expertise and practical understanding of technology. Media has tremendous impacts on the level of education. It is amazing to see how the internet is changing people's lives. People are able to quickly do research and gather data on the web, navigate through websites. Thus, the media plays a dominant role in learning processes.

Business houses have realized that they can use social media to generate insights, stimulate demand and create targeted product offerings. It improves business reputation. It also helps to build communities. Job candidates who develop skills in the latest and most advanced social media techniques are far more employable.

Negative impact of media on society

When we analyze the impacts of media it is a fact that mass media have a lot of negative impacts in our daily life. It is blamed for promoting social ills such as:

a. Cyber bullying: Teenagers have a need to fit in, to be popular and outdo others. This process was challenging long before the advent of social media.

b. Lack of privacy: stalking, identity theft, personal attacks and misuse of information are some of the threats faced by the users of social media.

c. The vastness of social media ensures that there is no control on the scope of information. Such situation can make people log into obscene harmful or graphic websites that may affect their thinking pattern.

d. Waste of time is another important issue.

e. Too much use of social media can affect a child's ability to develop wrong inter personal relationships.

f. Personal data and privacy can easily be hacked and shared on the internet. It may cause financial loss and loss to personal life.

g. Social media can easily ruin someone's reputation by creating a false story, fake news and spreading such falsehood across the social media.

h. The impact of social media on personal relationship is growing fast. One of the effects of social media is encouraging people to form and cherish artificial bonds over actual friendship. The term 'friend' as used on social media lacks the intimacy identified with conventional friendship, where people actually know each other, want to talk to each other, have an intimate bond and frequently interact face to face.

i. Social media is affecting the way kids look at friendship and intimacy. People are unable to differentiate between real and factual friendship.

Conclusion

It has been said that information is power. Without a means of distributing information people cannot harness power. One positive impact of social media is the distribution of information in today's world. Platforms such as Facebook, Twitter, WhatsApp and others have made it possible to access information at the click of a button.

Everything in the world has two sides, positive and negative. The use of media is no different. Its' pros and cons are decided

Anju Rose, SABS

by the users themselves. People are more isolated than before in the present world. Some make their world better by using media and others make themselves more isolated and immoral after using media. In all cases, balance and prudence is the key. The need of the hour is to train the people to use media effectively.

Ecological Concern: An Indian Feminist Perspective

Anju Teresa

Many attempts have been made to trace out the connection between women and nature. Scholars have come out with multiple opinions. It is clear from various discussions that the connecting factors are manifold.

The most characteristic of all qualities is their being the supreme generative entities. Both nature and women embody life-giving and nurturing virtues within them. So the representation of nature as mother is not altogether accidental.

Correlations can also be seen in the ways in which women and nature are exploited. Eco-feminism sprouts from the basic assumption that oppression of nature and the subjugation of women are directly related. Patriarchy which is founded on the male/female binary also distinguishes between human and non-human. In such a social structure both are undervalued and often treated as resources to be utilised at the will of men; they are hunted, harassed and are deprived of their dignity.

In the Indian scenario, the link between the women folk and Mother Nature is much more domestic as the rural women depend upon natural resources for their very survival. Women play essential roles in their management as they fetch water, pick firewood from the forest, and collect fodder for domestic animals and so on.

Agriculture has a decisive role in defining social structure and gender roles in India. Women's contributions in farming sector especially in horticulture, sericulture, fisheries, food processing and other allied activities are widely acknowledged nowadays. Along with her household chores, she manages to produce agricultural crops, domesticate animals and collect fuel, fodder and water. She may also work in agricultural land for wages. But quite often women are underpaid and are exploited.

Through farming and related activities women get closer to nature. Unlike men who look at natural resources as things to be commercially exploited, women tend to see them as resources required for their sustenance. An emotional attachment emanates between women and nature. It also puts her in an advantageous position as she acquires profound knowledge of environment, its resources and the degrading forces. Rural women possess amazing knowledge about herbs and natural medicines.

The closeness with nature makes women more nurturing and caring towards it. In an era of environmental degeneration women should step forward as the major actors in movements for the protection of nature, for the problem affects women the most.

India has recorded successful environmental movements initiated by women. The Narmada Bachao Andolan (NBA) under the leadership of Medha Patkar is just one example. It did not go unnoticed that the active participants of Chipko Movement of 1973 were the poor womenfolk of hilly regions.

Women can actively engage in afforestation programmes. In articles accounting the Chipko Movement we come across descriptions of free planting sessions of the movement. Such activities helped in the protection of a number of rare species. The rise of self help groups in the countryside have resulted in increasing awareness of the need of afforestation and forest conservation activities.

Women are the central figures in the management of water resources. Water resource depletion affects her the most. The changing climate and depletion of ground water level have alarmed women of the gravity of the issue. Under MUNREGA women undertake water conservation activities such as well recharging, rainwater harvesting, watershed management, well construction, and so on.

Women being aware of the need of soil conservation have taken initiatives for contour ploughing and controlling shifting cultivation. Through self help groups, women have entered into constrictive activities like organic farming.

Today a large number of women appreciate the use of unconventional energy sources. Women have become wary of the consequences of the use of conventional energy sources. Seminar and classes by self help groups and other governmental organisations have helped in raising awareness among women. They have started pressing for investments in solar energy panels.

Solid wastes pose serious challenges, particularly in Indian cities. Often these are dumped callously into rivers. But women voluntarily undertake to manage the waste being conscious of the health hazards, the undisposed solid waste may cause.

Over the past five decades, Indian History has recorded the names of inspiring women leaders and successful movements on the ecological front. The 1700, Bishnoi Movement in the Marwar region of Rajasthan led by Amrita Devi protested the destruction of the village's sacred trees. The Save Silent Valley Movement in Palakkad district in Kerala started in the year 1978. Acclaimed Malayalam poet-activist Sugatha Kumari played the lead in the protest.

The Narmada Bachao Andolan, most noted of its kind in 1985, was a protest for not ensuring rehabilitation for those who have been displaced by the Sardar Sarovar Dam Construction. Medha Patkar, the social activist, raised her voice against the injustice meted out to the poor people.

The Chipko Movement by its very non-violent nature had become a rallying point for many future like-minded movements. Also engaging in constructive activities like tree planting, it laid down the fundamental principles of ecological movements. The poor, rural women of the Garhwal region of Northern India embracing trees to prevent them from being cut down attracted worldwide attention.

A major player in the eco-feminist movement in the national and international levels, Vandana Shiva argues that the shift from subsistence farming to commercial farming accelerated by the Green Revolution has been disastrous for the Indian agricultural sector. She has suggested that more sustainable farming practices can be ensured by engaging women in the field. Eco-feminists like Vandana Shiva undermine hierarchy and acknowledge the intrinsic diversity in nature and the interdependence between the so called human and non-human worlds.

The shared experiences of subordination and exploitation, the sense of being the 'other' can be channelized productively so that these emerge as a concern for each other between nature and women. The division of labour based on gender has put women in nourishing and caring roles. A protective figure, close to nature women can well address the key environmental issues and contribute to environmental rehabilitation.

The Healing Touch

Aparna Thomas

American author Leo Buscagila says, "Too often we underestimate the power of a touch, a smile, a kind word, a listening ear, an honest compliment, or the smallest act of caring, all of which have the potential to turn a life around." From the day man and woman was meticulously moulded in the hands of the Almighty to this era of multi-dimensional explorations in technology, there lies an untouched power of dexterous hands; the power of touch – the primary language of compassion and a primary means of spreading compassion. They are the ligatures that bind humanity. But today, the pain and misuse of touch has created fractures in humanitarian attitudes of the human family. Understanding the philosophy and the power of touch by exploring its role in the spiritual, physiological and psychological realms will be a productive step to resolve many of the crises of this new era.

Touch is a cardinal virtue in spirituality. It is an integral part of Christianity. In an article entitled 'The Sacrament of Touch', theologian and author, David Torkington, rightly points out that the heart of the gospel story begins with a special touch. It is the touch of God, when the 'finger of God's right hand' touched the Virgin Mary. She conceived through the power of the Holy Spirit so that the love of God was made flesh within her womb. As God's Word, Jesus 'grew in wisdom and understanding' under the influence of the love that had conceived him in the first place, he was able to communicate with others by his sacred touch.

Jesus' choice to heal through touch, especially when the religious leaders of the day did not seem too fond of touching, was remarkable. With few exceptions, he either laid hands on those who sought healing from him, or they touched him. In Matthew 6:2-4 a man with leprosy kneels before Jesus and says "Lord, if you are willing, you can make me clean." Jesus reaches out to the man and touches him. "I am willing. Be clean!" Certainly, Jesus touching a leper was not appropriate in those times; yet it was the 'right choice'. It was a compassionate choice, and the man was healed. Touch begins with compassion.

It was the grace of healing through touch which was the ultimate symbolization of Jesus' love and compassion that was handed over to the apostles that not only gave physical healings but also inner transformation. This is why touch is so important in the rite of Christian initiation. There are theologians who even consider touch as a sacrament.

The impact of touch is astonishing in human physiological aspects. Skin that senses touch is the largest organ in our body. Neuroscientist Edmund Rolls points out that touch activates the brain's orbitofrontal cortex, which is linked to feeling of reward

Aparna Thomas

and compassion. There are studies showing that touch signals safety and trust, and it soothes. Basic warm touch calms, and activates the body's vague nerve, which is intimately involved with our compassionate response, and a simple touch can trigger release of oxytocin, aka "the love hormone". Studies also say that our hands have the healing positive energy to cure the pain of our body parts. Above all, the touch of a mother, the hug of a friend, and the pat of a well-wisher, are all touches that have great influence in our lives.

Devi Shetty a cardiac surgeon from Bangalore shared in an interview about the power of touch. He says that the power of touch is phenomenal. The moment you touch a patient, that creates a feeling of confidence in their hearts. It has larger healing power than all the surgical tools and medicines available in the world. Unfortunately, the power of touch, compassion and caring is gradually losing ground. The power of touch has various psychological interpretations too. Touch is the first sense we acquire and secret weapon in many relationships. People can impart and interpret the non-verbal modality called touch. In 2009, Depaw University psychologist, Mathew Hertenstein, demonstrated that we have an innate ability to decode emotions via touch. It is a powerful language which has no script or grammar but can be understood by the whole of humanity.

Today, the language of humanity is subjected to abuse and exploitation. The alarming increase in the number of rapes, barbaric murder, drug abuse, terrorisms, mob lynches and all the associated issues are the results of the 'abuse of touch'. We belong to a country that has marginalized a group of people as 'untouchables'. This kind of prohibition of touch, the God given language of humanity in the name of caste, disease, gender are grave attacks towards our humanitarian qualities.

Y and Z generations today claim that they are connected to each other across the world, but how far can one genuinely understand or express their emotions and feelings through emojis and virtual images? One can say that the sheer attempts to develop the 4D, 8D and more dimensions are the result of the inner quest of the human beings to reach close to the human experience of touch which they terribly lack in the virtual word.

It's high time that we understand the power of touch, the language of compassion, the divine expression of the degrading humanity. Humankind is moving towards that level of development where they have big houses, small families, more degrees, less common sense, advanced medicines, poor health, touched moon, neighbours unknown, high income, less peace of mind, more knowledge, less wisdom, costly watches, no time, above all more humans, no humanity.

The concept of touch is not confined to a few conventional physical acts. It is not to be misinterpreted in association with sexual connotations and cultural diversition. It comprises a wide horizon of human actions that contribute new dimensions of meanings to our existence on this planet. When our lives run behind the bandwagon of hectic schedules, technologies, hullabaloos of media and our day to day pains and problems, somewhere somehow we cast aside our inherent onus to 'touch' and to 'feel the touch'.

The philosophy of touch is facile. It asks to be the reason for others to smile, to give that pat of sincere appreciation, to be that comforting hand, to console a broken heart. And that is the philosophy that nature, world religions, and even science strive to teach us. Touch begins from compassion. It is the expression of compassion that accomplishes our existence and human beings, the creation that was made out of God's special touch. Spread it.

Non-resident Labourers: New Natives of Kerala

Ashly Paul

What happens to a plant that gets replanted to a new soil, to a more conducive environment? What is the reason why birds fly from one continent to another to feel comfortable in more friendly climatic conditions? It's all about moving and going places, in pursuit of better prospects. Living beings are blessed with the innate ability to move. Nature too asserts its agreement with the need of movement; the nature conditioning that enables human beings to step beyond fixed boundaries.

Migration is a very well etched concept in the history of humankind—be it the Exodus of the Israelites from Egypt to the fecund land of Canaan, or the migration of Joseph and Mary with baby Jesus from Bethlehem to Egypt. Bharat or India was conquered by the Mughal Emperors, as a result of which it saw the arrival of artists and a certain population, to the rich land from the Islamic nations. 'America' or 'New England' was the consequence of the settling in of the discontent Englishmen of Britain, migrating to a new land. History gives evidence of many similar instances of migration.

Indians are always trendsetters when it comes to migrating to foreign lands for better standards of living. This is evident from the estimates of the Indian population abroad, the Non-Resident Indians (NRIs) in the Gulf nations and other countries like USA, Canada and others. Migration is viewed as a livelihood strategy. In more recent times, globalisation has accelerated the movement of Indian peoples to other nations. Among the Indian states, a considerable number of people from Kerala have opted for international migration. This wide gap left by the Keralites in terms of man power for labour and development is adequately being filled by the influx of needy labourers from the other states of India.

Kerala: A Migrant's Paradise

Kerala has indeed proved to be God's own country for the migrant labourers who come to seek better means of livelihood. Internal migration had been on a rise in Kerala, owing to the 'safe' image that Kerala showcases. This has been a blessing to the state itself that was in the grip of native labourer shortage for skilful works. As per statistical data, the migrant labourers from different states constitute about 10% of the total population of Kerala, i.e., about 33 lakh people. Every year, the migrant worker population in Kerala increases by 2.35 lakh people. They are, by now, a significant economic force in the state.

Migrant labourers have been pouring in to Kerala from states like Tamil Nadu, Karnataka, Odisha, Jharkhand, Bihar and West Bengal. Migration from Tamil Nadu is a matter dating back to many years as they find it easier to identify with the language, structures and systems of Kerala. Despite the wide differences in the linguistic, social cultural aspects of Kerala from other states, the rush of the migrants has been very strong.

What makes Kerala one of the most sought after destinations in the country? There are several factors that answer this question. Kerala offers the best wage rates than any other state in the country. A construction worker earns Rs 700 on an average for a day's work. The good wages give ample opportunity to the labourers to lead a decent life on account of a moderate cost of living in Kerala unlike in Mumbai and other metropolitan cities where income for menial jobs is very less but the cost of living is extremely high. The high wage rates and sustainable job opportunities have made Kerala the right pick for migrant labourers. Kerala offers political stability and a comparatively peaceful environment for their survival. Political unrest in some of the North-Eastern states drive the people away from their homeland and some of these find solace in Kerala and settle here. Kerala is noted for its religious harmony; and hence, is a safe ground for Christian and Muslim migrants.

Yet another attraction is the socialist leaning of the Kerala model of development. Some of the migrants who have come to Kerala with their families cited the availability of better educational and health facilities as an additional impetus for living here. The Government of Kerala is in a process of framing several schemes and policies to uplift the social standards of the migrant workers.

The fundamental rights in the Indian Constitution provide for free and compulsory education for children up to the age of 14. The children of the migrant workers get enrolled in

Ashly Paul

government schools in the state, where they are also taught to read and write Malayam. In addition to this, the state educational department has set up more educational centres under the *Sarv Shiksha Abhiyan* (Education for All). The Government is also planning to set up certain skill development institutes for the workers. The Indian Institute of Infrastructure and Construction in the Kollam district is a progressive step towards this cause.

Kerala is the first state in India to enact a social security scheme for migrant workers. The state offers free healthcare for all migrants in government hospitals. In 2016, a new insurance scheme called *Awas* was launched to provide social security to them. In 2017, the Government announced a health insurance policy which included free treatment worth Rs 15,000 and medical insurance with accident coverage. They have been made part of the *Rashtriya Swasth Bhima Yojana*. The 'Migrant Suraksha Project' extends its support in giving awareness on the need to live healthy and protect themselves from communicable diseases. The Health Department of the state is planning to establish help desks for the redressal of the grievances of the migrant workers.

The migrant population in Kerala is mainly concentrated in the districts of Ernakulam, Thiruvananthapuram and the Malabar region. Migrants arrive in Kerala from other countries like Bangladesh and Nepal. Though these workers form a significant segment of the working class strata who provide for the economic growth of the state, there are a few issues and challenges that are to be sorted out. A major problem looming around is the involvement of the migrants in criminal activities. Many migrants are accused in different criminal cases such as fake currency dealings, robbery and drug trafficking. Investigations that found a migrant as the prime suspect in a sensational murder case in Perumbavoor in Ernakulam district adds to the notorious activities in which they are involved.

The contribution and role of the migrant workers in the construction of the Kochi Metro Rail can never be forgotten. The pillars of the Metro Rail stand strong on the sweat and day and night toil of the migrant workers. Another matter of interest is a migrant worker from Kochi who played notable roles in two Malayam movies delivering his dialogues in Malayalam.

It is always challenging to accept a foreign land as our own, especially when the social and cultural aspects are starkly different from one's own motherland. We often call the migrant workers 'bhai'. Let it not be used just for the sake of addressing, but it should bring out the true meaning of brotherhood. The current situation in Kerala is a reminder of the 'consumerist' approach to everything. The children of the highest literate state cross barriers moving to newer landscapes and their absence is filled by other Indian brothers and sisters. The migrants often face an identity conflict and the disturbances of dislocation and relocation. Let us shed the concept of 'the other'. Empathy gives meaning to our existence. Let us make the plan of God reverberate in our actions. We come as guests; but, we shall leave as a family.

Ashly Paul

Social Customs and their Influence on Women's Education in the Contemporary Context

Ashmi Mary Mathew

*"A nation's culture resides in the hearts
and in the soul of its people."*

Mahatma Gandhi

A custom is a law or right or usual way of life, which is not written, and is in practice since a long time. It can also be called a tradition. It is anything which a lot of people do, and have done for a long span of time. The meaning of culture is also similar to the meaning of custom. A custom is more about practices; while culture is the way people live their lives and it's more about ideas or a cluster of customs.

Kerala is the land of panoramic coastal beauty having a unique continuous tradition of assimilated cultural trends which developed through centuries of contact with the outer world. To study about the customs and the speciality of Kerala there are many components to be taken into consideration. The land and its people, myth and mythology, religion and society, customs, ceremonies and rituals, festivals, oral literature, music, dance and theatre arts are some main elements to study in order to understand the cultural identity of Kerala.

The role and behaviour of women in every society is determined by social structures, cultural norms, value systems and social expectations. Norms and standards of our society do not change at the same pace as changes take place due to technological advancement, urbanization, cost and standard of living, growth in population, industrialization and globalisation. Even in modern times, social and educational policies fail to cope with desired changes in various fields. Particularly, the social status of women in India is a typical example of the gap between the position and role accorded to them by the Constitution of India and the restrictions imposed on them by social traditions. What is practicable and possible by women and useful for them is, in fact, not within their reach. They have to exist within the framework of social norms and standards, which in turn cause infinite harm.

Women are an indispensable part of society. Education is the first step in the mending of our future. Kerala's social customs have been altered by education. Education has brought many changes in society. The patriarchal mode of thinking had been adversely affected by education. Education struck a blow to our customs and culture. Educating women can have an influence on coming generations. The development of the future generation mainly depends upon the education of

Ashmi Mary Mathew

women. Hence, the education of women is realised to be the most essential part of the development of society. It can help every woman to educate their children to be good managers of the family as well as active members of society, at large. The children learn their manners and good behaviour at home; and, understandably, mothers are mostly responsible for cultivating good behaviour in their children. Every educated woman can think well about her future and her aim in life and then choose the appropriate subject which will be useful to her throughout life. Education of women results in qualitative improvement of families and societies.

Caste, religion and other customs have created many barricades for women. Women were denied a chance to mingle freely within society. At times when powerful customs prevailed, women were denied the use of all their potential to promote the betterment of society. But when our customs were confronted with modernisation, globalisation, civilisation, everything began to change. People started to think out of the box. Female children were also given some basic education; and, in a fast-developing and technologically highly equipped contemporary world, women also began to contribute their own ideas. When a chance was given to them they made their mark in every field of activity. When our customs and religion tried to subordinate them they broke the chains of the customs and they fought for their freedom. Finally they are now considered as a valuable counterpart of the male. All that they wanted was some space to prosper and promote life. But our religious and social customs were a reason and cause for their regression. The advanced thinking of some people—especially that of the Christian missionaries who thought out-of-the-box beyond rigid customs—has paved opportunities to many women to attain education and enrich themselves and others around them.

In history we can see the stories of oppressed women. Historically, most of these came as a result of policies within churches and organised religions. Thus, on the one hand, forced marriages, oppressive ideas about sexuality, quashing of rights to speak, and lack of stake in family and church leadership are all issues women have faced throughout the centuries; while, on the other hand, research in recent decades has shown that women who are involved in religion report higher levels of happiness. While religion can be oppressive to individual and gender rights, the Christian religion has, nonetheless, helped to pave the way for social changes and civil rights. Scriptural injunctions like: "There is no longer male and female, for you are all one in Christ Jesus" (Galatians 3:28) have instructed wives and husbands to have love and care for each other. All these paved the way to change the thinking of patriarchal society and protect and encourage women to work for society. The Protestant reformation helped change paradigms about views of women by first emphasizing the value of the individual, and one's own value in the eyes of God, a key underlying idea to the exploration of human rights. Hence the church is a means not only for building peaceful homes but also for empowering women, economically and educationally.

Mother is the first tutor of a child. From birth to school age the home environment and association of other members of the family plays a significant role in developing proper attitudes among children. Therefore it is very necessary that a mother with good qualities acts as a guide. Thus, the education

Ashmi Mary Mathew

of women is of great importance in our social life. It is the duty of society and government to provide adequate facilities for the education of women, because if we educate a girl, we educate the whole family.

There is a Chinese saying, "If you wish to plant for a year, plant wheat, if you wish to plant for 10 years then grow trees, if you wish to plant for 100 years educate your women." This indicates the importance of education for women. Napoleon said: "Give me an educated mother and I shall promise you the birth of a civilised nation."

Without educated women a nation cannot expect a high growth rate and solution of internet problems. Women and men are equally treated before law. However, our cultural conditioning is the main source of atrocities against women. Culturally a woman in India is supposed to remain confined at home for internal domestic routine work; while men, by contrast, are the bread earners.

A social custom is any form of expression or identification that masquerades as personal but is anything but personal. Amazingly, many people copy a pattern, behaviour or act thinking that it is "me being me" while it is really a social custom that has been adopted and imposed.

We Keralites had developed our own culture through the ages. We are the most flexible characters, who are ready to accept the culture of other people who have mingled with us. But at the same time, our forefathers were keen on framing a culture of our own based on Indian philosophy and Indian thoughts. We are ready to incorporate all the good aspects of alien cultures with the high moral values of Indian thoughts.

With the emergence of modernism and global culture, our views were changed. We were attracted to the western style of life. It brought about innumerable opportunities and scope for expansion. Our contact with the western countries is the chief factor in mutilating ethnic habits of our society. Colonial rule had affected the material life and social behaviour of the people and their mode of thinking. Colonial remnants are still being followed and can be seen in every nook and corner of our life. Qualitative education had also come here as a result of these influences. Education was offered to everyone including girl children. When the coloniser tried to impose their culture and customs, the adverse effects had merits in the education sector. In the earlier days, our customs restricted women from having education. But when culture was subjected to reforms, our customs were reduced to become simpler. Customs need to be preserved as they are peculiar property that animate culture. However, customs have had both negative and positive influences in our society. "Culture makes people understand each other better if they understand that their neighbour is, in the end, just like them, with the same problems, the same questions" says Paulo Coelho. In similar tone, Marcus Garvey has said that "people without the knowledge of their past history, origin and culture are like trees without roots." In sum, on the one hand, we should preserve our culture, and on the other hand, we ought to use it for the betterment of our society and world.

Jesus Christ:
The Rebel or The Religious?

Cerin Babu

History dates 14th century as an era which saw a revival of learning and thought – an age of Renaissance. The period witnessed the rise of free thought, logic and rationale. Dogmas were questioned. Ideologies were challenged. Conformity to local customs and rituals were no more appreciated. The Renaissance man and woman wanted to know the 'how' and 'why' of things. Great visionaries, philosophers and people of science were killed. People were burnt at the stake because they wished to retain and hold on to their identity. Many lost lives in their attempt to gain perspective. It was time for a great paradigm shift.

Thoughts along these lives however revert us to a time even before the Renaissance when the birth of a great visionary changed the denomination of time. Beginning from the conception till the crucifixion, the Bible gives us instances which show the divinity of Jesus Christ, the Son of God. He is the Messiah, who was born to redeem humankind; He is the fruit of virginal conception and a fulfilment of prophecies in the Old Testament. However, due to a sense of anthropomorphism, we tend to describe Christ as the Jesus of Nazareth, a Jewish carpenter, a teacher and a rabbi. The description makes him sound more familiar to the lay faithful.

Attributing human qualities to Jesus calls forth a further analysis of his persona which should include a discussion on his attitude towards the existing social order, His teachings and his take on religion, rituals and customs of his time.

There is always a clear distinction between the concept of 'being spiritual' and 'being religious'. One cannot be treated as the synonym of the other. Spirituality, in simple terms, denotes the state of a person who is conscious of the Spirit. One feels the presence of the supreme-being, acknowledges it, contemplates it and makes it a part of one's life. Such a person does not consider rituals as the absolute communication to God. One does not limit oneself to the confines of any religion rather attempts to find the presence of the Divine of everything.

Religion, by contrast, presupposes the need for rituals, perhaps on the pretext that the abstract nature of the Supreme Being makes it difficult for ordinary people to focus on their prayers. Hence it should be made familiar and most human-like. It also bases itself on the idea of being part of a greater community with certain rules and guidelines to follow.

The New Testament, on the one hand, portrays a society rooted in religion and rituals so much so that rituals gained more significance than society. Jesus, on the other hand, gave little importance to rituals. He often refuses to fast, offer prayers or observe obscure Sabbath stipulations despite being warned by the people. He hates the hypocrisy of people and is bold about voicing his opinion.

He questioned the Mosaic Law and the social order of the Pharisees and accuses the Teachers of the Law for not entering the house of knowledge, while, at the same time, preventing others from entering as well. He chides them by saying that they are fine tombstones for the prophets thus revealing the social intolerance towards men of knowledge and wisdom prevalent during the time. The social disposition was such that they were complacent and intolerant so much so that they opposed any new strain of thought. In their midst, Jesus was in fact as outcast in terms of his thoughts and personal stance on issues. He accepted anything and anyone who was rejected by society. The best instance is that of him forgiving a woman accused of adultery (John 8:3-11) asking the men who condemned her to look into their own self and repent for their sin.

Never being confined within any dominant ideologies of the time, Jesus gave voice to his own speculations. He criticized the social order without giving much thought to the context or being afraid of the audience.

Disciples called Jesus as the Rabbi because he taught and talked to people in parables. Parables are usually defined as simple, short tales with a moral. It is easy to read and understand a parable. However, one will realize that Christ's parables cannot be considered as simple short stretches of tales but rather they are deep and thought provoking and ones that call for multiple interpretations.

Gospels portray Jesus as a teacher who never imposes his teachings upon his disciples. His teachings were open ended in the sense that they invite varying viewpoints and interpretations. One needs a bit of critical sensibility to grasp the meaning of his teachings which he did expect from his contemporaries.

Had he been born in our times, we would never interpret him as a divine person but perhaps label him as an eccentric professing strange idea. It is difficult to label him as a particular character type but 'religious' is definitely not the appropriate adjective for him. He is the culmination of binaries – the divine and human, bold and subtle but far more importantly, spiritual and rational. He is a prophet who proposed a counter culture, a new way of life. Call him what you may, Jesus Christ is the founder of a movement that has grown from strength to strength over twenty centuries with close to two billion followers, worldwide.

Cerin Babu

Denying Empowerment: Gender Inequality in Education in India

Jess George

"If all men are free, how is it that all women are born slaves?" this famous quote of Mary Astell depicts the plight of women in society. Our society doesn't consider woman as equal to man. She is regarded only as a second sex. Gender inequality means the idea and situation that men and women are not equal. It refers to the unequal treatment or perceptions of individuals wholly or partially due to their gender.

Gender inequality is always seen in life expectancy, education, politics, salary and so on. This may be mainly based on the hierarchical system of society. In case of life expectancy, studies show that women had more life expectancy than men. And in order to calculate the access of education of both males and females many scholars organize various activities. In India, the condition of women's education is deplorable because there is unequal access of education.

Usually the difference between male and female is based on biological factors. But there are also some physical factors that distinguish each other Men are taller, physically stronger and very aggressive, while women are normally shorter, emphatetic and very loving. From birth women experience different environments throughout their lives. Society plays an important role in shaping the personality of women.

Another problem is the difference between the wages of men and women. This occurs because high risk jobs are assigned to men and they have different work experiences than women. Society has a tendency to lower the wages of jobs which are done by women. Men are reluctant to enter into female oriented works because of its supposed 'simplicity'. People consider some of the high risk jobs as deskilled because the particular works are authorized by women.

In case of politics, the numbers of nominated women are less than men. Women in politics tend to adhere to male standards. Power is always associated with masculinity. Women have less knowledge in politics than men.

In this article, the discussion is mainly based on educational inequality. Careful studies show that we should ensure that both boys and girls get education as an experience throughout their lives, rather than getting knowledge for completing a course. More girls than boys drop out of schools because of reasons such as minority status, early marriage and pregnancy, traditional attitudes, poverty, geographical isolation and so on.

Families with high income and assets are able to get better education. But a group of minorities and marginalized people exist across the world; they are downtrodden. These sections

Jess George

of people, mainly girls, are denied their right to education. The numbers of people that are not sent to school are people belonging to these categories. If there are facilities for education, it should not ensure security for girls. There is a chance of being tortured mentally and physically. For example, in the case of backward people, girls are sexually and physically abused by their male teachers. Thus, they discontinue their education.

Another barrier for achieving higher education for girls is early marriage and pregnancy. Among villagers, early marriage is part of their cultural practice. These customary actions often deny girls rightful education. Over the years schools did not provide the opportunity for girls who were married or for young pregnant girls. They did not support it because schools must ensure legal support. For this practice, married girls are forced to drop out of education for the career of their children, employment prospects of their husbands and so on.

The traditional attitude of society towards girls' education did not allow them to get higher education. These customs provide soft skill jobs for girls such as schooling, nursing, writing, cooking, cleaning homes, caring of children and so on. But men had the right to select any course they liked. They were free to choose jobs such as engineering, machinery works, mathematics, technological works, etc. Traditional rules say that women should stay at home and look after the kids, whereas men should go out to work and earn a living. Moreover, married women are often forcefully denied access to occupations of their choice.

Poverty is a common barrier which leads to dropout of education. Girls belonging to poor family backgrounds face a lot of difficulty to get education. In some cases parents send their children to any childcare organization to ensure their safety instead of sending them to schools. For low income families, child care is one of the factors in the family budget. Likewise, on account of poverty, parents send their children to work rather than to schools, especially their girl-children. Thus, they are also a part of family who access income. In the past, schools did not support noon-meal programmes and free uniform facilities. As such, children from poor family background in schools suffer from hunger and they become ill. Consequently, they stop their education.

The educational system discriminates between female from male through the process of choosing courses. Females tend to take service works such as nursing and teaching, writing and so on. But men tend to take technical courses such as engineering, technology, and so on. Women are led on different paths before they choose their field. Instead of choosing the path they are interested in, they forcefully follow the paths which are selected by their parents.

There is the hypothesis that gender inequality emerges from historical attitudes regarding the education of girls as well as certain parents choosing to prioritize their son's education over their daughter's education. This may be due to hidden opportunity cost of engaging girls in activities (e.g., childcare) that have economic value for the family, particularly for girls in rural areas and from the lowest income families.

Several factors influence negative attitudes towards the education of girls. One is to save dowry. Dowry system forcefully makes parents to take decisions to limit their daughters' education in order to save money. If their daughters get higher education, they fear that it results in having to pay higher dowry. Also, a misconception that only sons care for them in their old age leads them to invest money for their son's education, health, welfare, and so on, rather than invest for their daughters.

It is important to discuss how we can overcome educational inequality. In case of early marriage, every individual must try to stop early marriage that affects the education of children. Through awareness programmes we can discuss with women in local areas and overcome this barrier and provide a fruitful educationa. Schools should provide education for married and pregnant girls instead of denying them education. Also we ought to try to change the attitude of people towards married girls. Thus we can ensure their education.

Overcoming lack of confidence is one of the factors to address in order to stop educational inequality. A healthy sense of self-confidence leads us to face unexpected events in the working place and find solutions without any fear or tension. Confidence is the power that enriches our development.

The negative attitude regarding girls' education needs to change. Many movements have shown that women are not second class citizens. The proponents of such movements have argued for the right of women to work and have access to an equal income as compared to men. Women were also shown to be equally capable of working and competent in their work.

Nowadays we can see that more women are working than before. When they are at work, men also do certain household chores in order to help them. Women today are getting married in their early thirties—a little later than what was customary earlier. It is vital for every individual to ensure education and work for the bright future of girls and humankind in general. After all, educating a girl is tantamount to educating a family. Remember, the hand that rocks the cradle rules the world.

Good Samaritan Meets Transgender

Joyal Jose Panachipuram

'Good Samaritan' is a story in the Gospel which emphasises mercy and compassion. Jesus was not a mere story teller. Through this parable, he conveyed a theory of mercy. He actualised this theory on Mount Calvary by a shocking death in which he wiped our tears. He chose the best choice and he became the best choice; "If there are choices, choose the lost. If there are no choices, be the lost."

Who is a Good Samaritan? He/she is the one who responds positively to the problems of the other person. The Good Samaritan is an ideal. He/she is a fragrant rose in the garden of the Lord. A Samaritan becomes a Good Samaritan when he/she helps the neighbour who is in need. Who is my neighbour? Is it only my villagers? No. For a Good Samaritan, neighbour is the one who is at the proximity of existence. It is not a physical proximity but it is a proximity of my kindness. Whoever requires my mercy and attention is my neighbour.

Transgenders

Transgender is an umbrella term which includes any other gender which is not masculine or feminine. They are called as third gender, and in India we call them '*Hijra*'. While the Good Samaritan is an ideal, transgenders are more biological. Today transgenders are the most marginalised (untouchables for many of us), not because of their deeds, but because of their nature which was given by God. What are our attitudes towards them? Are we replicating the roles of the priest and the Levite by avoiding them? If we are to be Good Samaritans then our attitude towards them will include respect and acceptance. Our 'frames' of reference/view will be renewed. Through this article, I dream of the day when we become Good Samaritans to comfort the transgenders properly.

Transgenders: Human beings?

Survival of the fittest is the law of nature. But Christ promoted the survival of the weakest. He inspires us to go to the peripheries of society. He needs the deprived, oppressed, outcaste and the little ones. We consider transgenders as a microscopic minority as well as untouchables. Many of them are accused of theft, robbery and so on. Why are many of them thieves and criminals? They are thieves and criminals because nobody gives them a job. They are sex workers because they do not have a second option. It does not matter whether they are masculine, feminine, transwoman, transman and so on. What matters is that they are human beings, created "in the image and likeness of God" (Gen 1:26-27). They are to be respected and accepted as they are. They have equal rights of jobs, opportunities, education, and life styles. We ought to change the frame in which we

Joyal Jose Panachipuram

view them with prejudice and preconceived notions. Nothing is accidental, coincidental, but providential when one uses it in right way.

Transgender in the path of a Good Samaritan

"Be the change that you wish to see in the world." – M. K. Gandhi

"Hundred homilies preached can never match a holy life."

We wish for creative changes. Philosophically, every change is painful. But it opens a lot of chances for incredible growth. Let us imagine a way in which a transgender meets a Good Samaritan. The oppressed and 'outcast' transgender will surely find solace, and get acceptance and respect from the Good Samaritan.. Yes! We have got a new vocation: to be a Good Samaritan for TGs. They are also one of us. We have the same essence. We are the children of the same God. Let us be transformed as 'good samaritans' who are not a structure but a situation. He cannot be structuralised. It is a situation of open-mindedness at the same time being rooted in Christ. It is a *pravarthimarga* as well as *nivarthimarga*. Christ became one of us, he became little. Let us also 'be little' so that we will be able to serve the little. Be little, serve the little.

Even though there are various organisations for transgenders, we have to widen and spread their programmes. We have to become aware of them. We have to make the public aware that transgenders are one of us. They are not to be mocked, eliminated and marginalised. If we provide enough jobs and opportunities, they will be enriched, both in mind and body.

It has been said that 'smiles reduce miles'. Our attitude is important. Elegance is not an action but an attitude.

An eye-opening experience

'Experience is the best teacher'. Once I met a transgender for an interview. He opened his mouth. "I am a man, I have a penis. But I also have breasts. Is it my fault?" When I could not answer, he asked again: "Would you allow me to marry your sister even if she wishes?" I was totally silent; I felt trapped in-between the devil and the deep sea. That was a breathtaking moment for me. I was totally shocked. It caused me a sleepless night. This question continues even today. Dear friends, how would you answer him/her for the same question?

Through the Samaritan's perspective

"Look the bees upon the thyme; they find there a very little juice, but in sucking it, they convert it into honey, because it belongs to their nature to do so." – St. Francis De Sales (Introduction to devout life).

"If there are choices, choose the best. If there are no choices, be the best." – English proverb.

A little juice in the flower becomes honey when a bee touches it. A transgender is accepted and respected when S&he* is touched by a Good Samaritan. Giving each person his/her own due is justice from ancient Greek philosophy onwards. A Good Samaritan considers the help which he/she offers to a transgender as if it was his/her duty or 'dharma'. He/she bears

---

*There is no popular pronoun for introducing transgenders. I would like to form a pronoun from 'S/he' and it is S&he.

Joyal Jose Panachipuram

a hand, with an undivided heart. There happens as an accident of two hearts. There is a saying in English – "Bend on the road is not the end of the road. But it is a change of direction." A Good Samaritan finds possibilities amidst impossibilities. The Word became flesh and we called him Jesus. We need to become the fifth Gospel, a Gospel with flesh.

The book 'Treasure in Clay' of Bishop Fulton J. Sheen talks about two kinds of hunger. One is hunger for bread and the other is hunger of spirit. The latter one is satiated only through helping the needy. Transgenders are undergoing an identity crisis. They have to be rehabilitated. Their rehabilitation is impossible unless our viewpoint or frames of reference get changed. At first, we have to spread awareness among the public that transgenders are also humans like us. S/he looks into their eyes and says "you are precious". As Ambani influenced the whole India by the 'Jio' mobile plans, Christians shall be the new 'jio' for spreading the love of Jesus. Let our actions speak louder than any voice.

We need to be an updated version of Jesus in the modern world. Mary was regarded as a 'walking tabernacle' while she was pregnant. If I were regarded as a walking tabernacle or carrier of Jesus, how much bliss would I have? We are called to be various advertisements of Jesus. We shall make a butterfly effect of love and mutual collaboration. It will enable us to view transgenders as full human beings to be loved, respected and accepted. S&he is precious. Because S&he was called in divinity, with mobility and for dignity.

Nun: The Powerful Female

Karunyamaria, CMC

The word 'female' is constituted by adding 'fe' to the word 'male'. Therefore, it is a fact that female contains something 'more' than male. The theory of feminism started as a revolt against male supremacy, whereas now it deviates its path and enters into various vulgar forms. Real feminism starts with the awareness of one's strengths. God is love. God creates human beings in the divine image and likeness. Love endures through sacrifice and self-giving. Woman is the ultimate symbol of sacrifice and self-giving. Therefore, woman is a powerful being who is the bearer of life on earth.

While we talk about the power of woman, we should consider the real fact that 'a consecrated woman' or a nun is the ultimate powerful female. As she is 'alone with the alone' she is always free from the bondages of human relationships and its self satisfaction. She is united with God and the heavenly abode, which is the ultimate goal of human life. Freda Mary Oben points out, when she analyses the life and actions of Edith Stein as scholar, feminist and saint, "...both Christ and

Mary were made free from that dependency of relationship to another human being for the fulfilment of life's significance. This is replaced by the relationship of each to God: Christ through the hypostatic union, Mary through total surrender."[1] The power of woman lies in her role such as mother, bride, lover and initiator. We cannot replace anyone for these roles. In other words, woman serves the function of creator and redeemer. Without having any bondage, nuns freely serve these roles in their fullest sense.

Nun: The Real Mother

The most exalted vocation for all women is to win children for heaven. To give birth to children in Christ. A nun gives birth to God's children through her constant love, prayer and sacrifice. According to Saint Pope John Paul II's *Vita Consecrata*, "...Virginal love is the source of a particular fruitfulness which fosters the birth and growth of divine life in people's hearts."[2] Saint Mother Teresa of Kolkata proves this truth by giving birth to millions of God's children. The nun is able to change the world and go beyond all political power through her purified motherly love and concern. She has no obligations to some particular child like a married woman and is not bound to a family. The mother earth is her family and all human beings are her children. A nun has the power to go anywhere calling people as "my child" Her motherly affection, kindness, forgiveness and self sacrifice make her to be a fountain of love.

Nun: The Real Lover

It is indeed a feminine yearning for every woman to give herself completely to another as well as to be completely possessed but the other. But in reality no human being can really fulfil that yearning. Nun, the real lover, forgets herself in total commitment to God, and God's Spirit fills her soul. She is always waiting for her lover like the girl in the Biblical '*Song of Songs.*' She always meditates about her lover, reads and recollects his love letters (the word of God). She finds her treasure in God because her heart dwells in and is attached to God alone. As a lover who is always happy and enjoys life in its fullness, she drinks the joyful cup with her beloved. A lover's mind should reach out to the favourites of her divine lover, the poor and the marginalized. This offering is hailed as Jesus' thanksgiving to his Father in *Vita Consecrata*, "their offering, besides its elements of sacrifice and expiation, takes on the aspect of thanksgiving to the Father by sharing in the thanksgiving of the beloved Son."[3] Nuns burn always with this divine love even in the midst of sufferings.

Nun: The Initiator

A woman has the obligation to be the facilitator because she is surrendering herself for others. A nun as a powerful initiator should be the promoter and always the inspiration for others. Mary, the perfect model of religious, is the powerful example. *Vita Consecrata* quotes, "... in the New Testament passage which portrays Mary with the Apostles in the Upper Room... we can see here a vivid image of the church as Bride...there emerges above all the aspect of fruitfulness..."[4] A nun gives birth to God's children and at the same time she leads them to the right path, Jesus. Her self-consciousness and creativity make her to be the real guiding light for the future generation. As *Vita Consecrata* suggests, "Consecrated women therefore rightly aspire to have their identity, ability, mission and responsibility more clearly recognized, both in the awareness of the church and in everyday life."[5] A nun's primary mission is the formation of youth, as cells of the mystical body of Christ. Nuns, with their tender loving care, should turn the present day youth from their desperation, loneliness and fear which induce the use of drugs and alcohol, pornography and abortion. The nun is able to enter into the psyche of the needy ones and understand them as lost sheep. She is the real initiator to turn them towards our merciful and compassionate God.

Nun: The Real Bride

Marriage is the experience of belonging completely to another person.[6] A married woman has the limits to feel free with society, whereas the nun is able to dedicate her whole life fully for the redemption of people because she belongs to the Great Redeemer. Nuns have a special power for good in public life because they are brides of the great revolutionary. Mary, the Bride of the Holy Spirit, appeared publicly in the most dramatic confrontation between good and evil: the crucifixion. Nuns must become involved in modern burning issues. Like a bride, she must always brood over the desire of her bridegroom. Jesus is the face of God's mercy. His bride must reflect this face in society. The nun has the opportunity to be alone with her bridegroom in her deep hours of meditation and is able to personally converse with Him. She will be able to imbibe his will and be a wellspring of love for His Kingdom. A nun transforms her physical needs into spiritual satisfaction that emerges from social services. She has the feeling of oneness with the perfect being, thus she can elevate her existence to the heavenly abode. *Vita Consecrata* asserts that – "...consecrated men and women are also called to a 'transfigured' existence."

Conclusion

Vita Consecrata says:, "By virtue of their dedication lived in fullness and in joy, consecrated women are called in a very special way to be signs of God's tender love towards the human race and to be special witnesses to the mystery of the church, virgin, bride and the mother." Without a virgin, a bride, a mother, the world is powerless and incomplete. A nun is a powerful woman living life in its wholeness. The realization of the self and its manifestations helps her to dedicate herself absolutely for evangelization. She needs to break social boundaries and taboos to eradicate fear and inferiority. A nun, the awakened woman, has to inspire the world to wake up and be joyful for the peace of the world.

Endnotes

[1] Freda Mary Oben, *Edith Stein: Scholar, Feminist, Saint*, Alba House, New York, 1988, 46.

[2] See his Apostolic Exhortation, *Vita Consecrata*. Carmel International Publishing House, Trivandrum, 2005, 486.

[3] Ibid., 510.

[4] Ibid., 486.

[5] Ibid., 508.

[6] Pope Francis, *Amoris Laetitia*, Saint Paul Society, 2016, 278.

Do You Really Need the Fan? Some Reflections on Conservation Habits

Linda Therese Luiz

There was a time when my mother would save each plastic cover and rubber band and keep each unused piece of paper to be made use of later. We have moved 'on' from that thrift economy. Today it is not the lack of matter but rather the overabundance of matter in the form of 'waste' that has become our issue. All of India is grappling with this menace at present. Yet a contradiction is that we are concerned about the *management* of waste but somehow we are not giving as much importance to the *generation* of waste. Why is this so?

Today we see the growth of production, the proliferation of commodities and corresponding to it, the large-scale increase in waste. Waste is a necessary outcome of a capitalist, consumer economy where consumption and even wastage are encouraged. Waste becomes inevitable under this system. If one were to question the production of commodities above and beyond our needs, one would be questioning the very logic of capitalism itself.

The Ease of Wastage

In feudal and monarchical times, conspicuous consumption was an important marker of status and privilege. But today wastage is something that is taken for granted by all, a 'right' that comes to us from the money that we pay for a commodity. If thrift made economic sense earlier, today wastage makes sense under the same system, now that commodities are available freely and cheaply. Today we waste because waste has become convenient. It is convenient to use and throw, to buy a disposable carry bag at the store, or to simply throw a cheap half-used paper into the waste bin.

Our commonsense tells us to consume because it makes life easier. By the same token conservation becomes difficult when we internalize the principle of wastage. This is quite obvious in terms of certain habits like buying chocolate – you buy it because you like it, but you are not conscious of the waste you are producing in terms of the wrapping, the energy spent on its creation and transportation from the original place of production. You can get around this problem by opting for locally-made items that may not involve as much packing – but these items have lesser shelf-life, and may not look as aesthetically pleasing or as comforting as the familiar colours in which your favourite chocolate comes wrapped. It is simply more convenient to buy branded commodities because of the matter of familiarity (not necessarily because of proven quality).

Linda Therese Luiz

Wastage is not simply with regard to material articles that we buy, but also with resources such as water and electricity. Electricity is not as dear a commodity as it was perhaps a generation ago, and so wastage has become much more common.

The Difficulty of Conservation

It is easy to suggest that one should take up alternative means instead of what one is already accustomed to. But why is it difficult to change? One part of this may be attributed to the fact that we all have 'recipes for living' – methods that have come to us as a result of previous experience which help us get through much of our lives without the need to think. Therefore even if we are conscious and reflexive with regard to some aspects of our existences, we are unthinking about many others.

How many of us, for instance, think about the necessity of the fan or the air-conditioner? There are many who are so used to it that it has come to occupy the stage of inevitability. Yet we may recall times when it was not considered inevitable. One generation previously, these may even have been luxuries. While we can all argue for the comfort these electronic appliances provide in extreme temperatures, let me cite one example – what does it mean when people close their doors and turn on the air cooler when it is pouring heavily outside? If one were to allow the coolness in the outside atmosphere to permeate into the house one would not require an AC or even a fan, at times. But our daily habits are too out of tune with the rhythms of nature for this to happen, and we are hardly conscious of this.

In Kerala it is a habit of many people to enter a room and immediately switch on the fan. This is understandable given the relative humidity in the atmosphere that makes one sweat when one has undergone some exertion. The fan is a means to get rid of the sweat and feel cool. What one does not realize is that often in the same situation, given even a light breeze, if one were to sit for a few minutes the sweat would cool by itself through evaporation, allowing the body to cool down in its own time rather than requiring an outside agency to manage it.

There are some who like to put the fan on at full speed and then wrap themselves in a blanket. Though it may sound adorable, this is actually a very unsustainable and wasteful practice, also one that significantly increases the power bill. Human discoveries have helped us go beyond natural devices but the question is, how much is necessary? Especially in an age when we are thinking more and more about conservation of energy and various resources, we need to ask ourselves, how much can we do without?

What Can We Do? The Individual's Response

Is it possible to go to a stage of less consumption? It would be possible but the change will have to be on multiple fronts – from the macro-perspective of institutions to the micro-level actions of individuals.

At an individual level we could each examine our habits. Consider the tap that you turn on. Most taps have variable water flow, but nobody gives attention to it. What we don't realize is that the more water is allowed to come out, possibly the more water is wasted. One must thus become conscious about waste in our daily lives – from the fan on a cold night

Linda Therese Luiz

to the packed snacks we consume, to the *chai* we leave at the bottom of the cup, our habits can make the difference.

The Institutionalization of Conservation

Some years ago serving of refreshments to the Chief Minister of Kerala in a steel cup at the opening ceremony of the National Games held at Trivandrum was highlighted in local newspapers. The state of Kerala has been actively taking many symbolic and practical steps to encourage a sustainable lifestyle among people. Indian administrators are becoming more and more conscious of the need for efficient waste-management strategies. The 'Swachh Bharat Abhiyan' is an important initiative in this regard.

How can the Church contribute?

At one time in Kerala monasteries and convents owned large tracts of land, 'green spaces' with emphasis on agriculture and other primary activities including cattle-rearing. Keeping up with the times, Catholic institutions, especially educational institutions have been quick to embrace various principles of environmental conservation and 'Green Protocols'. The propagation of environment-friendly and waste-reduction strategies through schools and colleges is a potent tool for influencing the next generation. But more remains to be done, in the construction of churches and associated buildings and in the enforcement of sustainable practices especially for functions that are held within church premises. Restricting or preventing the use of plastics, restricting the use of disposable items and promoting the use of reusable plates, glasses, water tumblers, etc. is quite within the ambit of the Church.

Finally, what about the light and the fan?

Construction is a very important sphere where principles of energy conservation can make a lasting impact. The Government of India has come up with the Energy Conservation Building Code (ECBC) with guidelines for the construction of energy-efficient buildings. Today we hear that the Cochin International Airport Limited is fully solar-powered and energy-neutral, drawing power from the solar grids installed in its grounds, a model Kerala can be proud of.

Some of these principles can also be adopted by individuals and institutions. If the very design of buildings is environment-friendly then the need for artificial cooling or artificial light in the form of tube lights reduces. This is an important principle of energy conservation. Often houses are constructed with the provision of windows but they are kept closed, or the light is obstructed by the use of heavy curtains which necessitates the use of artificial lighting inside the house even during the day time. Some houses are planned without adequate cross-ventilation which means the occupants have to pay the electricity bill on account of the fan for years to come.

Not only do we incur costs in this manner, but we are also passing up the opportunity to feel the rhythms of the breeze or to hear the sound of insects and birds which chirping when the fan is on at full speed... often we have the choice. What would you pick?

Linda Therese Luiz

Emoji – The New Language
Maria Sharol

In this 21st century, beginning with the mainstream usage of emails and other instantaneous messaging Apps, people are finding better and more effective ways of conveying their emotions and opinions. In this era, we get anything and everything we need in a few seconds. We have everything at our finger tips. The fast growing world along with technological developments have brought tremendous change in popular culture. Each year we get to know about new developments and technologies. These technological developments influence us tremendously and they also work as a medium for communication. This essay explores how 'emojis' influence us, and how the use of them could act as better channels of communication.

Emoji or emotions are faces, usually using characters of language, which express emotions, often animated due to their popularity. The word 'emoji' originates from Japanese. Earlier they were called 'smileys' and 'emoticons', but now they are usually referred to by the term 'emojis'. This word was added to the Oxford Dictionary in the year 2015, and was declared as the 'word of the year'. The whole world now commonly uses the word. These were first installed in Japanese phones and later were installed into iPhones and Android operating systems.

Now let's take a tour on how emojis influence us or in what ways we are dependent on them. In this era, there are many ways of expressing our thoughts and feelings. We could just express them by showing our different moods to the world. People often use these innovations as an advantage. There are many ways in which emojis help us to convey our thoughts very easily.

There are some good and perfectly valid reasons behind 'emoji-ing'. They have a great emphasis on public posts, online and other social media sites. This could even change the way to communication. We are able to communicate faster with the use of emojis. We can express an idea or viewpoint by simply using an emoji showing different moods. People are trying to make up their own rules as they go. It is completely organic.

The usage of emojis has been one of the greatest challenges we face for writing. With increase in the use of emojis, people have stopped writing; they find emoji-ing an easier and more effective way of conveying their thoughts through different moods. However, emojis too have certain limitations. These emojis can easily be misinterpreted. This is because there is no specific definition to any of the emojis provided. We often assume and come to different conclusions when we see emojis. The main issue which we face is the cultural and contextual interpretation of images. Different cultures interpret different emojis in unique ways. Some may even consider these emojis as a means of mockery towards their culture. This might also lead to disputes and discord. The second challenge we could face is that people could become lazy; they might often use short-hands or entirely different languages which the receiver might not know. This can also be a challenge towards writing.

Today's youth are deeply influenced by the use of emojis. They even fall into the habit of using emojis just as they develop their own slang. This has become a major problem in society. Even small children have fallen for this; they too are attracted to this easier way of communication. A research has found that 72% of 18-25 year olds somehow find it easier to communicate their feelings and thoughts using emojis rather than using words. This is likely the case with young children too. The research was done by Cambridge author Vyvyan Evans.

Now, let's see: how do emojis work? We normally generalise emojis as faces which express emotions. But, going deeper we realize that emojis help us to produce tone and body language; otherwise our communication will be a plain text. A plain text cannot create any emotional or major change to the sentence. However, if we add some emojis it enhances our expression. These can be considered as an alternate way to convey nuances; and to some extent, these could enable us to showcase our ability and affect an emotions or thought across languages and cultures. Indeed, these emojis are a mixture of emotions and icons.

The increase in popularity of using emojis have pressurized its creators to add additional emojis. Nowadays, we can get anything and everything in the form of emojis. We now have not only facial emojis, but we also get dialogues as emoji. In various messaging Apps, dialogue from different films can be used. These things make communication easier. Time is not wasted typing plain text when we can download them and put them wherever it's applicable. This has a great impact on popular culture. In fact, certain emojis have been recognised globally. "The face with tears of joy" was the most popular emoji across the globe. There is also a division in the emoji between the regional and social dialect.

Texting is not only about private messages between two or more groups of people. It is something which is globally accepted. Social media like Facebook, Twitter and Instagram give us platforms to go live across the world. People express their thoughts and feelings, which go live on the globe. If we express our feelings on plain text, they would just be pieces of information or meaningless thoughts. But, if you put a smiley face on that post, then the idea can easily be conveyed. Suddenly, the message becomes interesting and people take notice of what is communicated. These emojis can also be used as an indicator for irritation over political context. A political issue may somehow irritate human beings a lot; their expression can be conveyed through emojis. For example, if we think about the 'cow protection' (*gau raksha*) movement put forward by the Modi Government, this topic brought out a sudden change in society. Many people expressed their views through putting emojis and other relevant opinions on the topic.

If internet or social media were platforms for plain text and bland expressions, they would have very little attraction to people. However, if we add some expression to ideas, we would be attracting the whole globe. We also find that emojis are a

Maria Sharol

medium of communication with people who are differently abled. They easily get the ideas or the emotions conveyed. The differently abled people communicate through emotions; they see things and understand the ideas behind them. The emoji system can be very much useful to differently abled people.

Nowadays people text a lot more than they talk. The portrayal of emotions is very important and of great significance; and these are unavoidable when talking person-to-person. Voice inflections, facial expressions and body language all portray what you mean by what you say and your responses of what is being said to you. Regular words can't match that; simply typing out how we feel is hardly efficient. So emojis are important and widely used.

Browsing through this essay, we realize how much our world has been digitalised and how we have got a new language – the emoji. Today, the emoji can be considered as a universal language. We all use emojis in order to express ourselves. The facial images play a subtle role in society. We now get an idea of how far these images influence us and how we are dependent on them to convey our feelings and expressions. In the digitized world, the use of emojis has become a major element. They play a crucial role in our society. How else will we make everyone understand what we say?. We should be able to convey what we are thinking. It's said: 'actions speak louder than words'; one might even say: 'emojis speak louder than words.' That's is why you and I use emojis.

Post Satyagraha to Post-Truth

Naveen Joemon

O f all the truth seekers known to us, Gandhiji deserves a unique position. It is not because he named his autobiography 'My Experiments with Truth', but the uniqueness of the Mahatma is that he embraced a practical, lived-in dimension of truth, which he termed '*Satyagraha*'. Contrary to the Gandhian experiments, the icons of our era have experimented divergently with truth. This climaxed in the extermination of the real, better termed as 'Post-Truth'.

'Post-truth' is the Oxford word of the year 2016 and till date its rise has been 2000%. Post-truth is defined as "relating to or denoting circumstances in which objective facts are less influential in shaping public opinion than appealing to personal and emotional belief". Etymologically, '*Satya*' is derived from '*Sat*' which means imperishable. But contrary to it, the very foundations of truth are crumbling today. We live in an era where the political leaders and corporates deploy the technology and media for shaping public opinion and create, 'pragmatic truths' that suit their interests.

Post-truth makes a new phase of celebration of the unreal, where the very foundations of democracies and nations are shaken and debilitated by populist institutions. All across the world, the post truth era is witnessing an outright rejection of truth, amplification of hollow electoral promises and the eclipse of reality under the darker shades of populism. 'Post-truth' trends were very evident in the US election, Brexit and in media stories even from India.

The tech savvy generation finds a cosy niche in the world of virtuality or in the security of the bubbles provided by the cyber world. Here it is not the matter of commoners who get blindfolded and consciously go by blatant disregard of facts, but the gyration of truth by the politicians well coated with elusive embellishments of emotion that forces the people to do away with truth. Thus, as a global trend, truth is stripped of its essence and falsehood is catered to with trappings of factuality. As a matter of fact the truth is in retreat.

Adolf Hitler's infamous aide Goebbels said: "If you tell a lie big enough and you keep repeating it, people will eventually come to believe it". It was the true strategy of the Trump propagandists. Some of their hoax stories are as follows: "Pope Francis supports Trump for election", "Trump offers free tickets for those who wanted to leave America to Africa", "ISIS leader extends support for Hillary Clinton", "Obama bans the pledge of alliance in schools" and so forth.

Such crooked stories could easily vilify the opponents and in this online spell, they entrenched public opinion. The hike in Facebook likes and Twitter hashtags deceitfully draw us towards "news" that we like. The acclaimed British journalist

Matthew D'Ancona writes, "the buzz of the hive sends the falsehood fizzing into cyberspace to do its work". This reminds us of the old maxim: "A lie can travel halfway around, while truth is putting on its shoes."

Lying in politics is not new. Plato ascribed to Socrates the concept of 'noble lie' that calls for social harmony and promotes civic devotion. But today, the lies have become so dominant that the conspiracy theories alone survive and emotions matter more than facts. Greek philosopher Salvoj Zizek says, "The reality is its own best semblance." Looking at the reverence for political lies, he is of the opinion that it is impossible to draw a clear distinction between deceptive reality and the positive kernel of the real.

The 20th century witnessed a paradigm of excessive worship of the real. But from this excessive reverence of truth, unfortunately in the 21st century we ended up with the tyranny of the post truth. An important question: Why are we so carried away by post-truth? The answer is falsehood no longer appears as a lie more real than the truth. So Jean Bauderllard writes, "The real is suffocated by its own accumulation."

An important ramification of post truth is that politics has degraded from contest between ideas to a contest between 'news and polls'. D' Ancona writes, "The normal practice of political debate is morphing into an unhealthy relativism." The voice of public opinion is no longer just, no longer authentic. The treacherous industry of lies pronounces election verdicts and public opinion as dictated by political leaders.

The unprecedented hike of post truth is credited to the development of social media and technology. Social media has

Naveen Joemon

taken over the world and is redefining it. The effect is that the speed of connectivity is also the pace at which we take these fabricated lies for granted and are not willing to test them. These have never been a more efficient modus operandi to spread a lie than to post it online. Social media has blurred the distinction between the real and unreal, between fact and fiction, between truth and untruth.

Citizens are simply deceived by the post truth and worse is the fact that they suffer for their foolishness. After subscribing to lie factories, citizens reward them with political success and become their obedient subjects. Philosopher Jean calls this "voluntary servitude". The futility of their votes and folly of their political positions would only occur to them as a late realisation as it has been with Trump and Brexit.

The global analysis of the political undercurrents in different countries would give us the crux of post truth. D'Ancona says, "Post truth politics at its purest is the triumph of visceral over the rational, the deceptively simple over the honestly complex." But one should not equate post truth to political lies and spins alone. The problem is more with the lukewarm and vulnerable response of the public with the deceitfulness of the politicians. Instead of denial and revolt, the reaction was simply that of acceptance. Post truth instead hoodwinked the citizen's power of political deliberation and commitment to truth.

It has not been long that the word 'post truth' has been circulating in Indian tabloids. The Indian intelligentsia have started to bring out parallels and similarities of the post truth ramifications in India as against the political tremors in the US and UK. Post truth has become an accepted category to highlight the widespread worry of the common folk, troubled by their government and politicians. Communalisation, reconstruction of history, ecological plunders projects, antagonism to refugees, modern caste reformations and so forth come through the channel of post truth.

It is clear that post truth hoaxes and circulations are politically motivated. Their goal can be best expressed as social smuggling, a word coined by Kancha Ilaiah. A political formulation in the outset of post truth could be as, 'a process of exploitation where it means earning political success by manipulating public opinion and not investing back into the society by fulfilling the political promises'.

At the root of the issue is the moral deterioration of media which has become a mouthpiece of post truth agents. The fourth estate of Indian democracy has metamorphosed into a lapdog instead of being a watchdog. The celebrity mania, media trials and fake stings are post truth in colour and odour. Important areas of enquiry are shut down and not aired.

On the other side courageous journalists who bring out the truth, risking their life are rare. One such was Gauri Lankesh who was silenced forever for indulging in a warfare with post truth constructions. In her last editorial, Gauri Lankesh attacked at the duplicity of the media and ridiculed them as "Gibbelsian lie factories".

It is time that truth is rehabilitated. Courageous journalists and inspired youth must take the lead role to bring forth and birth a current Satyagraha. In the face of conspiracy theories, the desire for truth, Satygraha, is the only solution. Let us retrieve those Gandhian weapons for the modern war of independence.

Naveen Joemon

The Increase of
Social Media Trolls in Kerala

Naveen Thomas

In this nuclear era, the social, political, religious, cultural issues are discussed through social media. It is an open platform to express an individual's freedom and thought. There is no other medium which is so effective and efficient. It has the option to have open discussions on topics, far ranging and varied, expressing one's feelings regarding different ideas and the freedom to critique the elected government. In this day and age, with the saturation of social media to such a degree, sharing one's ideas and opinions and having people react and respond to them in real time is a reality that none of us can wholly deny or escape from. One of the effects of the spread of social media and real time reactions of opinions is the trolling and meme culture.

Humor is a popular tool for online trolls, most of which are only good natured ribbing meant to entertain and possibly help the uploader tweak their future uploads accordingly, but inevitably quite a few of these trolls happen to be vile and juvenile attempts to hurt or incense others. Online trolls help to collect the response of people. Everyone is free to create trolls and everyone can access them. Trolls are part of culture and art. Trolls have become very much part and parcel of social media platforms like Facebook, Whatsapp, Instagram and Twitter.

Online trolls can be considered as the newest versions of humorous revolutions like Kunjan Nambia's "Thullal". Later, it was seen in movies and mimicries. 'Ramanan' and the roles played by Salim Kumar has great impact for the development of trolls in Kerala. There were many interpretations for the scenes of different movies. There is always a quick response to the incidents that happen in Kerala. Many are not ready to protest or share their experiences in public; they convey their views through these trolls in social media. Even though trolls are just for infotainment, sometimes they engender a lot of controversies. Trolls can be only considered as imitations of the real incident because in most cases, they are half baked information.

ICU and Troll Malayalam are two prominent online forums in Kerala where decisions and comments are made. There are many other online forums which target the unwitting and spread untrue and unreliable information that then becomes generally accepted, which is a big red flag because this can lead to big issues later. Thus, the trolls try to manipulate or hide the facts from users. Most trolls relate with current issues, are easy to read and understand as it is in a capsule form. People no longer read the newspapers as they have become lazy and their lives are hectic; therefore, this can lead to a pessimistic influence among the citizens.

Naveen Thomas

Unlike earlier times, if we see something happening that contradicts our beliefs or toes the line of good taste and decency, we have the option to respond to it immediately. Social changes have been achieved because of people being able to voice their discontent with the actions of those wielding power. Big and mighty people have been brought low when people brought their vile or insensitive ideas or actions to light. Indian politician Kummanam Rajasekharan is the victim of the above-mentioned situation. Due to his appearance at the inauguration of Kochi metro, social media started to troll him. Because of that incident, a new word 'kummanadi' was formed in internet, which means 'attending a social event without having been invited.'

Trolls are used as a medium to promote and destroy certain things. Taking into account the Kerala scenario, movies are rated on the basis of trolls, which sometime pass wrong information to fulfil others' desires. Elections, *harthals* and so forth are discussed on this forum which can make a difference in society. Every minute incidents and actions are taken into account due to the mass influence of online trolling. The users and readers digest what is written in the trolls, whether it is right or wrong. Such thoughtless and harmful ideas can lead to a lot of dilemmas in the social milieu. Personal harassment and bullying is a major problem due to the effect of online trolls.

With the rise of meme culture, humour and sarcasm is laced with clever word play and funny images to offer criticism. Most times, they are socially relevant critiques, commentaries on current political climate or playful fun pokes at celebrities or politicians, but there is a darker underbelly to this culture. The recent incident of Sheela Kannanthanam, the wife of

Alphons Kannanthanam, can be taken as an example. She was responding to a media channel and at the beginning of the interview, she asked the reporter whether he had started recording her conversation. The reporter replied that it was not being recorded. So, Sheela started to talk in a casual way to him. Later, it was telecasted in a media channel and social media took over. Sheela was trolled in many ways. Troll images and troll videos were made on that 'interview'.

Trolls are sometimes misused by many just to satisfy the users and to show the innovative style of the person. Nobody needs to reveal who created the troll, as it could be from a fake account. Exaggeration is the real problem. Very silly topics are nowadays debated which have no significance in society. The impact and influence of social media trolls is vivid from the presidential election to college elections. It is also true that people read certain news after watching a troll related to that particular topic. One out of three who creates trolls is a youngster. Only a person who has knowledge and creativity on a certain issue could create trolls. Thus, it is true that the budding youth are well aware of the current affairs.

The trolls in social media often overstep limits, and the credibility of these trolls becomes questionable. Online bullying is one of the worst forms of trolling, where unfunny and often times cruel intentions of the trolls are used to attack and humiliate persons or communities. There are a lot of trolls that focus on pornographic content that drags society, especially the youth to a pathetic situation. Profiles dedicated to nothing but trolling others, most often without a shred of a sense of humour or social conscience have become nothing

Naveen Thomas

short of a menace. In Kerala, the significance of social media trolls has turned political. The present incidents are example for the prominence of this online trolling.

The increase and acceptance of political caricatures in newspapers is also a reason why social media trolls have increased in Kerala, as they have the freedom to express themselves. Freedom of speech is necessary but what we also need to establish is a safe environment where the freedom does not encroach on the liberties or lives of others and affects them detrimentally. Attacking anyone for their beliefs is unwise and regrettable especially where done with malice and misinformation. Trolling, when done right, can be an entertaining and socially relevant way to offer constructive criticism with use of humour and sarcasm, but with anything else, having censure and a sense of ethics that stops it from becoming vile and cruel with only malcontent and malice as a driving force should be stopped.

If the trolls in social media are presented in an optimistic way, it can lead to positive change in this modern era. It is true that in Kerala, trolls are mainly used to degrade certain people, this attitude should change. The creation of trolls should be for the betterment and upliftment of society. It should be an impetus to all and ameliorate present scenario.

Social Protests through Cyberspace

Neenu Jose

The title of this article will perhaps evoke some pondering. We often hear the term 'cyber crime' but we rarely discuss the positive aspects of cyber space. Cyberspace is a floor of interconnectedness where individuals share any kind of information. Clearly there are chances of misuse. Still, cyber space has paved its path for very successful social movements too. Social protests through cyberspace have always been a matter of concern. Many social movements have achieved active public support through cyberspace. Hence, the topic is of great significance in this digital era.

A vivid example of successful intervention by cyberspace is that of the 'Jisha Murder Case'. A thirty year old law student from Perumbavoor in Kerala was brutally raped and she couldn't achieve complete justice; even in her death. Cyberspace, as a whole, reacted to this brutal crime and exposed the police officers and others who were complicit in this crime. The inefficiency of police officials in reaching out to the culprits had been a matter of concern all over the media. Finally, blogs were opened urging for "Justice for Jisha". Many write-ups too were published. Altogether, the movement became vibrant, active and effective. Thus, cyberspace became a floor for expressing social protests in the Jisha Murder Case.

Moving on, another notable intervention by cyberspace was in the actor abduction case. Some months ago, a renowned Malayalam female actor was brutally assaulted. Following this, vibrant protests emerged through electronic and visual media. Cyberspace reacted vigorously towards the issue. Social media discussed the topic in great detail. Finally, quick actions were taken. There were many misconceptions regarding the investigation pattern. But violent aggression from the part of the public made the team conduct the investigation more sincerely. Participation of the public in this matter has been praiseworthy. And this was made possible only with the strong backup of cyberspace.

November 8, 2016, marked a special day in the history of the Indian economy. Our prime minister announced that notes of value 500 and 1000 would be withdrawn overnight. People heard the news with a kind of foreboding, and in the following days, India witnessed great confusion and chaos. People rallied around wondering what to do next.

In this context, cyberspace explored various possibilities. As responsible citizens of a democratic country, we too have power, the power of an individual and the power of organisation. Cyberspace tried to explore this great power and thereby did wonders. Facebook posts and tweets against this unexpected move made everybody react. Only massive movements have achieved success, both in the past and in the present. The posts and tweets were expressions of the people regarding this very quick social movement.

Obviously, cancellation and withdrawal of the larger denomination notes from the economy has brought changes. However, the major motive regarding the curtail of the flow of black money still remains unfulfilled. The widespread responses that emerged through cyberspace have helped in reducing the impact of the withdrawal. This happens because active social responses make the Government more responsible in correcting their mistakes.

Yet another important intervention would be in the field of social welfare. A matter to be discussed in this scenario would be that of the "Me too" campaign. It is an online social movement. In this movement many women came forward (female actors) to react against the sexual assault they encountered. Now, this small initiative has spread throughout the world. The response is tremendous. Many of the female actors came forward revealing their experiences of harassment in Hollywood.

The campaign has received widespread responses from different parts of the world. This is a great example of how social protests could be successful through cyberspace. India is a democratic country. We are all subjects in a democracy. And since we are subjects in democracy, we too have a say in building up a secular democracy. Politics is often a matter of discussion. Political parties play a crucial role in building up the nation. However, what is seen today is something that will easily ruin the nation.

Neenu Jose

Social protestors have often tried to criticise the political leaders with regard to their current political stand. Trolls play a major role in criticising political leaders. Not only political leaders but almost all those who are engaged in various arenas are criticised using trolls. So here also cyberspace has provided a platform for expressing the social protests.

So, trolls are yet another key for expressing protest. Here, too, cyberspace plays a key role. Tweets by celebrities and famous sportspersons have always played a crucial role in moulding public opinion. We are all very curious to see or know what celebrities do. Often people try to imitate them. Clearly, their opinions have a powerful and persistent effect on people's opinions.

Former Indian cricketer Virendar Sehwag is very active in social media. He is an ardent tweeter. Most of his tweets are of social relevance. They tend to express his attitude and stand regarding many issues of common interest. Recently there were tweets about someone who made negative comments about India's famous badminton players - Saina and Sania. He reacted vigorously against those who tried to hurt nationalist ideas or patriotic feelings.

When a famous personality like Sehwag makes his opinion clear through social media, then surely, he becomes an inspiration to many young aspirants. The opinions put forward by actor Kamal Hassan too have also evoked public interest against social evils. The interventions by cyberspace in resolving these problems are creditworthy.

One of the major advantages of using cyberspace is the fact that it helps to overcome obstacles of participation. Nowadays people spend long hours engaged in social media; and hence, cyberspace ensures large scale participation. Social movements become successful only when they have enormous public participation. Thus, the issues put forward through cyberspace are successful since they ensure a huge number of participants.

Many online social movements have also raised voices against the marginalisation of Afro-Americans. They consider cyberspace as a platform for expressing their aggression against institutionalized racism. Facebook pages are opened urging active public participation in many social problems. The dilapidated roads in 'God's Own Country' are a hot topic being discussed in cyberspace. Although this social protest has not achieved complete success, cyberspace has made it possible for the issue to have a larger outreach. Political leaders were criticised for their ignorance. They should always stand by the people, for the people, but what they practice is entirely different.

There are many more effective interventions by cyberspace. Since the world is moving fast, so are the people. People spend most of their time on social media. The advantages of using cyberspace cannot be confined to the idea of a larger public participation. But it could be extended to the context of being useful since they charge no membership dues and have low cost of establishment.

Prior to the actor abduction case, female actors of Mollywood decided to launch a new idea of introducing an organisation WCC – 'Women in Cinema Collective'. The major motive of the organisation is to wipe out the physical and mental torture faced by female actors. They have opened a new official page in the name of their organisation where

Neenu Jose

they can discuss their problems and make others aware about their problems.

Following this serious undertaking, strict actions were taken against the culprits named in some cases. Social protest is the need of the hour and social protest through cyberspace is almost mandatory today.

There is a dark side for anything. Nothing is perfectly black or white. Cyberspace is a stage for interconnectedness. Primarily, this connectedness could be treated as a merit or demerit. The effect depends on how we, the users, use it. Cyberspace is a web, or more specifically, a spider web. Cyberspace seems to fascinate us all. It could be used for entertainment. There is nothing wrong about using cyberspace for accessing information to address noble and worthy causes.

Cyberspace must be elevated from the level of entertainment to that of 'infotainment' where there is a blend of entertainment and information. Rather than isolating the world of cyberspace to brutal cyber crimes, we must try to identify the positive aspects of cyberspace. Everything has its own positives and negatives. The ultimate result depends upon use, as well as the wisdom of the users. Active social movements have achieved their aims and ambitions through prudent use of cyberspace. It is the need of the hour to switch over to these new methodologies for expressing our opinions regarding many issues.

Some Bytes on Bites

Rachel Berkumon

Who doesn't like a morning walk with a cute puppy? The answer would certainly be an enthusiastic 'Yes', whether you're a dog lover or not! But what if your walking partner were a stray dog? The very question contains two question marks with the issue of stray dogs becoming a larger question day-by-day. As silly as it sounds, dogs seem to have an upper hand in this whole issue. It is this intriguing aspect of this controversy which calls forth one's attention to the actual problems raised by stray dogs. This for sure will leave behind a long list of social, political, economic and ethical concerns that may sting us more painfully than any rabid dog bite.

The social problems associated with stray dogs can largely be put under the health category. A majority of the dogs we see on the street are lone wanderers with none to take care of them. So, with no timely vaccinations and health checkups, it is not surprising if some of these dogs are potential carries of the rabies virus. It must also be noted that a single carrier is sufficient to spread the disease to the rest of its pack. So where do you and I come into the picture? Well, the recent statistics prove that more and more humans are attacked by dogs without provocation, which indeed points a suspicious finger at rabies.

As far as we know, rabies is a cent percent preventable disease; but once it has affected someone, it becomes cent percent fatal. The many instances of human beings dying horrible deaths cannot go unnoticed at any rate. Hydrophobia and the likes of it prey upon many unfortunate victims who die without even a second glance from the authorities. However, the death toll of rabies is quite low when compared to other epidemics. Nonetheless its severity cannot and must not be overlooked. To add to the fear factor is the growth of aggressiveness among the once passive carnivores.

One cannot ignore the fact that the not-so-innocent dogs have started to find strength in numbers and hunt human beings like a pack of wolves. The shocking reports of the old, young and helpless becoming easy prey to a pack of violent dogs looking for dinner are a gruesome blotch on humanity. Moreover, the fact that a group of four-legged carnivores manage to keep the ever intelligent humans on the edge is a painful jab on our proud advancements. The social issues raised by the dogs point to our lack of interests in improving the waste management sector.

The inefficiencies in the management of waste and the associated pollution have an undeniable hand in the sudden hike in the number of dogs. The sudden acceleration in the population of dogs is found to be directly proportional to the increasing number of open dump yards and poor waste disposal.

It is quite obvious that there can't be successful breeding without proper feeding. The careless disposal of plastic bags containing food waste and the lack of waste disposal facilities in the cities are throwing back strong, well fed and 'ready to bite' dogs at us. This problem immediately finds its way to the top of the Government's faults and the issue takes a sharp political turn.

As for the political sides of the dog issue, the various stands taken by the Government at each level are equally conflicting. It is beyond argument that democracy values its citizens' life more than anything else. Yet, our celebrated principles are put to shame as the Government at different levels take different stands that most often have little or nothing to do with the welfare of people. What is even more disturbing is how the centre and the state Governments showcase their own agendas that do more 'backbiting' than dogs. They just try to come up with contradictory solutions which have a 'few barks and no bite' in them. Even in alarming cases when there is obvious endangering of human lives the solutions offered by the political power structures are either too broad to even consider or too narrow to accomplish.

The solutions offered by the Government come with an undertone that dog bites are not much a bigger problem than mosquito bites. The government solutions like castration of dogs are laborious, expensive and impractical with the rising numbers. The conflicting voices within political bodies about whether the dog is really a threat makes one wonder what is so good about a dog bite that it looks appealing to a few. To top it all off a man can get in serious trouble for hurting a dog while the dog is left on its free will to do as it pleases.

Rachel Berkumon

Many believe that the puzzling political stands have a not-so-invisible alignment to the hidden economic agendas of some. This is where the vaccine companies play the double role of hero and villain. It is not difficult to see their skills at fishing in troubled waters. While the unfortunate patients look up to the vaccine companies for a way out of their miseries, the vaccine companies in turn look up to the dogs to perpetuate the misery. With the unjustly skyrocketing vaccine prices and the artificial shortage of necessary vaccines in the market it is not offensive to think of the dogs being more humane than humans. Profit making and service are undeniably contradictory even when the companies manage to do both at the same time.

Profit making is seldom a one way channel. Therefore, quite a number of people are now turning their heads back and forth between the Government and the medical companies. As horrid as it can be, the possibility of a financial tie up between the two supported heroes is not far off. The accusation might be defined as a desperate attempt of the national brain to find the real purpose of denying justice to the helpless victims of dog attacks. But it is even more disturbing when the accused authorities fail to come up with better responses than a few wrinkled brows.

Lastly, the aimless four-legged carnivores roaming the streets raise a couple of ethical questions too. Both the dogs and human beings are indeed components of the same biosphere and are hence merely strands in the web of life. Human's superiority claims over another living being is now questioned by many at an ecological level. Even when the stray dogs are a menacing bunch the threat that they pose can merely be eradicated by shooting all of them dead turning a blind eye to the savage acts of dogs and the blind 'puppy love' of the so-called dog lovers is also not going to get us anywhere. What we need is a strategic and rational approach that starts eliminating the problem at its roots.

The cure can begin with the age old adage: 'Prevention is better than cure'. The solution that can remove the problem once and for all must begin with an H and end in another H, with the H's being hygiene and harmony, respectively. Clean environmental conditions and proper waste management can bring a drastic drop in the breeding rate of dogs. Then the stray dogs can be gathered up and put away from the public in places meant for the wild. There are several organisations that volunteer to take care of stray animals including dogs. Sterilization is another method to reduce population but it must be made more cost effective. The rabid dogs at any cost must be put to death immediately to save them and humans from further agony.

Finally, the Government and the people must come to a consensus to work for the welfare of their society and not for anybody's material gains. The idea of healthy society is incomplete without the last H being harmony where we treat the environment with more respect. This will solve the problems of pollution of waste that led to the problem of dogs. Thus, the issue of a bite a day can be narrowed down to blissful silence where dogs and humans draw the line of peace. So, let the wonderful morning walks resume without the fear of biting dogs that seldom bark. After all, it's 'all about a dog'.

Rachel Berkumon

Pros and Cons of Nuclear Family

Santhwana

In simple terms, a nuclear family system is a family structure that consists of two parents living with their children, also known as immediate family. According to Irena Shayk, "Nothing is better than going home to family and relaxing." Family has a vital role in moulding society. As society is made up of a group of people who belong to different families, the structure and nature of society basically depend upon the family.

As Michael J. Fox reflected, "A family is not an important thing. It is everything." The behaviour, lifestyle, character, discipline and everything is built up from the family. Hence, a family is the main factor which decides the good and bad of society. We don't choose our family. They are God's gift to us. Nothing outside ourselves will make us happy. The time spent with our family is precious, whether it is at work or at rest.

As a family, one can think only about father, mother and children. Also grandfather, grandmother, uncle and aunt may be included. Many believe that nuclear family is the best arrangement, yielding numerous advantages. However, with any system, there are disadvantages too.

Pope Francis's Apostolic Exhortation (*Amoris Laetitia*) on 'Love in the Family' the emphasises the Christian spirituality of marriage communion. He preaches that the Trinity is present in the temple of marital communion. Just as God dwells in the praises of his people, so does God dwell deeply within the marital love that gives him glory. The spirituality of family love is made up of thousands of small but real gestures. The mutual concern in family brings together the human and the divine.

Faithful to Jesus' teachings, we look to the reality of the family today in all its complexity with both its light and its shadows. A greater emphasis on personal communication between the spouses helps to make family life more humane. But neither today's society nor that to which we are progressing allow an uncritical survival of older forms and models. This is an evidence that, the principal tendencies are leading individuals in personal and family life to receive less and less support from social structure than in the past.

We must be grateful that most people do value relationships that are permanent and marked by mutual respect. Many are touched by the power of grace experienced in sacramental reconciliation and in the Eucharist. But there is a culture decline that fails to promote love or self-giving.

As family is more important than any other thing, we should think of the nuclear family over joint family where people in the past shared everything, lived happily in the midst of problems and sufferings from different areas. As we know, the joint family system promoted laziness among members of the family; yet, there were many good things in it.

Advantages of Nuclear Family

Nuclear family system plays a vital role in the overall expansion of character of individuals. Kids are more intimate with the parents and can frankly discuss their problems, which helps for the better development of their personality.

In this system, the condition of woman is better than in the joint family. She gets enough time to look after her children. She also gets time to plan and manage her house according to her own ideas and vision. There is no interference of elders. Husbands can also devote more attention to their wives.

There is more private space and freedom. The spouses have more free time to do what they enjoy doing. The members of a family have strong bonds among themselves. In short, each child in a nuclear family receives more parental attention and educational advantages, which generally raise their self-esteem. It is easier for both parents to combine careers with family. Family planning programmes become successful in nuclear families.

The children also benefit in the long run as they inherit property directly from their parents. Peace and harmony are very essential for a pleasant family life. In nuclear family, there is no misunderstanding and they enjoy a harmonious atmosphere by living together.

Here there is no shifting of responsibilities like in joint family. The parents are bound to take the responsibility for their children by themselves. There is no chance of in-laws conflicts. Financial problems do not arise. Money can be saved for future plans and for facing uncertain crises of the family. All enjoy independent life and engage in any economic activities to supplement family income. The will and desires of children are considered and are given proper weight. All members here are emotionally secure. No superiority or inferiority complex is felt by anybody. All are given equal weightage.

Autonomy is perhaps the chief advantage of a nuclear family. People can take decisions freely. Nuclear family has sufficient financial stability to provide luxuries and opportunities for children. They can pursue extra-curricular activities and activities like dance, sports, music or any other type of programme. With this they develop themselves socially and academically.

Though these are advantages of nuclear family, there are many disadvantages also. In this sense, the Holy Trinity is an example for the good and model for small family.

Disadvantages of Nuclear Family

The property of the family is divided among the brothers and each of them lives separately. On the one hand, the land being subdivided does not yield much production resulting in the land not being economically viable, and, on the other hand, one has to employ other labourers to achieve the desired goals due to limited size of family. In this way, the economic loss is more in a nuclear family by paying remuneration to the labourers.

Feeling of insecurity in children in the type of family is more. Here, both husband and wife choose professions outside the family, and then the children are often neglected and looked after by servants. They feel lonely and emotionally insecure. They develop more anxiety. In times of emergency, when accidents take place, and when women are pregnant, family members are much neglected and often there is no one to take care of them.

As it is an autonomous unit, it is free from the social control of elders. So the children are prone to develop all sorts of bad qualities like stealing and lying. They lead their life in an undisciplined way. They become more unsocial as they do not get the opportunity to mix with other members of the family. Feeling of loneliness is predominant among the members of nuclear family. After completion of household tasks, the housewife stays alone at home.

Like the insecurity of children, in nuclear families, the widowed, old and divorced often feel neglected. There is chance of family breakage in case of conflict between the spouses, since there are no elders to guide them.

Somewhere down the line, heritage and culture are lost as it is passed on to future generations. Chances are that they get totally obsolete in the process. With modernisation taking on the customs and traditions, it is apparent that the future generations will either have no knowledge of customs and traditions or they will be confused since they accept other cultures also.

The crucial problem that arises due to the nuclear family system can be realised when the child starts to get selfish. If devoid of that sibling relationship, the only child in a small family cannot learn how to care and share with others. Although the child can be involved in activities with other kids where he/she can study his/her social skills, it is not the same as the steady companionship that a sister or brother can give.

Children in a small family can become ruined and less accountable because as an only child in the family, he/she is habitually associated with ego and selfishness and develops less communal skills.

In conclusion, we can say that as there are advantages and disadvantages of the nuclear family system. Family is a place of sharing and caring. No matter how big or small, members of a family must live a happy life in all its fullness. Love must be the backbone of every family. This builds the strong pillars of love, caring and sharing.

Child Abuse:
A Grave Concern Today
Steffi Rose Babu

She saw each and everything with anxiety by holding the hands of her father. He introduced the world to her. Everything she saw was new to her. She was a little girl, as clear and pure as a crystal. She was not aware of bad or evil, as she was in the safe hands of her father. But some way she was stolen from the hands by some smiling face in the daylight. They made her a thing in their hand and used her as they wished. The pure crystal broke into pieces.

Abusing a child is as serious a crime as killing a person, because a child is tender by nature. Any abuse that she goes through in the primary stages of life leaves a lasting imprint in her mind for always. The abuse may be just for the enjoyment of those 'eleven minutes' but they are not bothered about the destructive outcome after the enjoyment. Not even about the mentality of that child or about the situation which she has to face thereafter. No ears were there to hear the screaming voice of the child, "Help me!"

It is hard for a child to erase such memories. Many of the victims may lose their confidence forever and live their lives as introverts. Only some may have the courage to fight and face the situation and rise up. We all are equally responsible for the introverted situation of these children. The attitude of many towards them does not allow them to mature. Once a sexually abused child will often face more than one type of abuse, as well as other difficulties in its life. Domestic abuse is another abuse which children are facing nowadays. Domestic abuse includes emotional, physical, sexual, financial and psychological abuse. Witnessing domestic abuse is really distrusting and scary for a child. It causes serious harm. It includes seeing the abuse, hearing the abuse, seeing a parent's injury and distress.

Domestic violence can happen in any relationship and even to young people. Many do not know what's happening to them is abuse; even if they realise it, they are not ready to reveal it to anyone as they are afraid or ashamed of what happens next. Age, race or gender doesn't matter for those affected by domestic violence.

It doesn't matter how much the child suffered the harm but whether the child suffered it or not. Whether it be emotional, physical, domestic or sexual, one out of four girls and one out of eight boys before the age of 18 is sexually abused in our society.

Religious freedom has become a point of contention. Some states allow for medical neglect due to religious objections. Emotional neglect includes withholding love or comfort or affection. Medical neglect occurs when medical care is withheld. Violence against children can be physical or mental abuse and

Steffi Rose Babu

injury, neglect or negligent treatment, etc. Violence may take place in homes, schools, orphanages, residential care facilities, on streets, in workplaces, in prisons, and in places of detention. Such violence can affect the normal development of a child, impairing their mental, physical and social being. In extreme cases abuse of a child can result in death.

Child abuse in India is often a hidden phenomenon especially when it happens at home or is done by family members. Focus with regards to abuse has generally been in more public domains such as child labour, prostitution, marriage, etc. Intra-family abuse or abuse in any institution has received minimal attention. This may be due to the structure of that family and the role played by children in that structure. Indian children are always dependant on their parents or elders.

It's hard to obtain the number of children abused in the home because most of those crimes go unreported. Sometimes social abuses are a result of poverty such as malnutrition, lack of education, poor health, neglect, etc., are all recognised in various forms by the Indian legal system. But it is the truth that there is no law specifying the protection of children abused at home.

The Constitution of India contains a number of provisions for the protection and welfare of children. It has empowered the legislature to make special laws and policies to safeguard the rights of children. Also India has signed a number of international documents and declarations that pertain to rights of children. Many treaties were signed for the upliftment of children. But being frank, it remains as such merely on white paper.

It is now our duty to think and act on it. Not beyond the law but what we feel is justice for us. As 'a bell is not a bell until someone rings it', justice cannot be justice until the deserved receive it.

Steffi Rose Babu

Specialising Tomorrows: Evaluating Education in India

Tarun Eldo Mathew

Remember the child you saw the other day; the one with questions about everything? Education has been helping us become refined. It helps us to be fit for society. And today, every society is a global society. Now, we have specialists in the field of education and healthcare. We are happily looking for precision and we are getting exactly what we want. But, what is happening to the larger picture, 'the grand whole'?

In this age of ever-growing expectations, every one of us is busy learning. Reductionism and analysis is everyone's mantra, the key goal. We see and hear things and are busy ourselves dissecting and scrutinizing—probing our consciousness into anything and everything around us. Education and the spirit of enquiry have landed us on great levels. It has 'enabled' us by giving us technologies. And with technologies, we survive. With technologies come problems and then comes technofixes: a cycle that will go on and on.

We have successfully established tech aids in our education system. With smart classes, broadcast televisions, DBS, in group forums, MOOCs and MOODLEs; education is more than enriched today. Patterns have definitely changed as seen by the change in syllabus now and then, the introduction of such systems as CCE, etc. Our educational systems have developed but there has not been an evolution. It is still similar to the one we had 60 years ago. Is holistic education going to be the game changer?

Tradition speaks for India when it comes to learning. There is a public misconception that our education system was established by the colonisers. It has been pointed out by a Malayali like myself, how our ancestors were studying in the universities of Nalanda and Takshashila, while the British contemporaries were busy hunting boars. The British did promote, or rather impose, education and set up educational institutions in India; but only to promote Britishness. Our ancient systems aimed at promoting knowledge. In the days of the 'Gurukul' system, the student would acquire both theoretical and practical knowledge from his master. The master was a full time teacher and a guide to his students. The student learned everything unbound by disciplinary boundaries. The case is very different today.

Today we are burdened by the availability of choices, and options are strangely limited. Information, and misinformation, is just a Google away. We tend to go for the virtual know-all teacher, as opposed to the teacher at hand: one trained with experience to give away the right information to the right seeker. Education today has become a race to gather information. We have all these data, but where is the wisdom, the insight we once had? Social structures and global structures expect one to

Tarun Eldo Mathew

gather as much information as possible. One apt example is the system of entrance examinations, often resulting in depression and suicides. And all are creative in their own unique ways! Today we often fail to link facts/information and end up with too much information and too little knowledge.

If not disabled by health or time, it would be unique to opt for an alternate school/university system. Distance education and correspondence courses have had tremendous upgrades since their inception but are not yet functional enough to replace the current mainstream system. The virtual world too has not grown enough, not to replace the current system. One learns not just books and is never limited to the four walls of a classroom. We gain a tremendous amount of values and friends and experiences from our schools and universities. This helps to mould a socially aware human with a heart; as opposed to a virtually fed logical beast, filled with information. Wisdom makes one humble enough to seek more knowledge and to care about others. The term holistic education has gained great prominence in recent times. It involves activities and projects along with regular learning to help mould a better human. It goes hand in hand with the current system of education and helps to evaluate co-curricular skills and EQ, along with IQ and everything of the regular order.

What should be the driving force, as one sustains in the system of education? It must be to seek knowledge and learn what interests each one. Although the education system restricted extra learning in the past, today it provides space for and encourages heterogeneous interests. Being first a third world country and then a post-colonial state, India and her uniqueness was being restricted. Today, we have reached a kind of saturation and are in a way done aping the west. We are on a serious route towards understanding and promoting everything Indian. We are beginning to celebrate our uniqueness everywhere. This is seen in the revival of age old practices, festivals and cultures. This revival of interests is happening on a fairly large scale. The focus of education is slowly beginning to mirror this change of interests. The new values instilled will help us love learning. Students will no longer come to schools and universities just for a degree. Schools and universities will not force anyone in the name of food and attendance. A genuine interest is being planted by the very evolution of the Indian society. And the wind of a new renaissance is beginning to be felt.

Education and learning provides a platform for all, especially the oppressed. We have witnessed the rise and the subsequent acceptance of several such groups in the past. These include but are not limited to African Americans, feminists, communists and more. Literature has been the playing field for the ideas and views and dreams of the oppressed, the marginalised and the downtrodden. In India, it is education and the awareness created by education that helped the Dalits come out of fear and stand for themselves. Today there is tolerance and acceptance of Dalits. Although there are cases of Dalits being mistreated and offended, the rate of assaults have come down on a drastic scale. Education is proving to be the cure for Brahminical hegemony, where both the oppressors and the oppressed are victims of a system. Dalits have found a platform to voice themselves in literature. And Southerners, such as myself, understand them through the same platform. Maya Angelou said of how the caged birds sing of freedom. But others can only understand the song

Tarun Eldo Mathew

if one is familiar with the language or the patterns. Education provides a common ground for discourse and interaction. It levels out all the hierarchy and serves as a platform fit to express.

The relationship between religion and science is a widely debated topic. Religious texts, figures and experts have given us a fairly great amount of knowledge. Formal education is focussed on mainstream sciences. Religion is believed to deal with abstract ideas and science with facts. In reality, both religion and science deal with both facts and abstract concepts. We often come across contrasting content on comparing religion and science. Thus, many assume of a cold-war between the two institutions. But religion does not oppose science; in fact the true essence of religion provides ample space for sciences and deconstructive ideas. All religion asks for is to be rooted and to be open. Pope Francis supports the Big Bang Theory and a lot of top level scientists are highly religious. Religious virtues and values we gain from education go hand in hand with each other. We are, today, surrounded by educational institutions set up by religious institutions. They are open to and cater a secular crowd. This is a good example showing us how religion and science can co-exist together.

As Bacon said, what we learn is fine tuned by experiences. The holistic approach of education aims to help us choose judiciously and to be emotionally and intellectually open to new learning. An orthodox mind is only focussed on what it knows and is intolerant to new and especially opposing ideas. Today, we are socially wired to choose and read books and articles on the basis of trust calibration and coherence. To grow and evolve one needs one's intellect to be tickled and questioned. Modern education is providing works, which have the potential to give shell shocks to the thoughts and assumptions of a student; thereby moulding the generation towards a better tomorrow. With the application of theories and isms of all kinds, one is shown various perspectives. Soon one learns to think deep and wide and beyond the boundaries of these theories – to think out of the box. Thus, a world of new prospects and possibilities opens to them.

The Regulatory Board of the Indian Educational Council has been vigilantly altering the system to provide better and feasible education to everyone. There has been a constant endeavour from their part since the 1980s. There are councils of expert academicians, scholars, subject experts and language experts who work together at aiming to improve the overall vision of the young generation. Various elected governments, over the years, have introduced a variety of schemes in association with various organisations and institutions: to provide better education to students of all classes, creed and race. Student text books and other provisions are provided at the best quality and the least possible cost. Student exchange programs are being promoted to help students get first-hand knowledge of both Indian and foreign culture, customs and tradition. It also shows the measure of openness to the 'other' and helps cultivate the wisdom to share and exchange knowledge.

Education as a noun is merely passive. But as it becomes a verb, it gains certain dynamism -- quality of vitality. There are definitely shortcomings in the system, but education aims at elevating students above and beyond the constraints of the system. Thus, education that does not make a change is not

Tarun Eldo Mathew

living to its purpose. When knowledge leads to crimes and the systems within education are forcing students to go through mental stress, education is failing. Lack of job opportunities and the need of better qualification as the years go by are a direct result of India's uncontrollable population. Education can help solve this issue by creating awareness. Be rooted and be open, as wisdom comes from everywhere. Let us be ready to question. Let us welcome changes and revolution in the realm of education lest it be filled with evils, like in stagnant waters. Education alone may fail to provide morality and morals may exist outside formal education. To make the best out of education, one must approach it with extreme care and caution. Learning, like praying, is very personal and must not be imposed upon anyone. Religious values can be expressed effectively through the words and deeds of an educated mind. Today the Gurukul system is being redefined in the form of research guides, student exchange programs, conferencing virtually, etc. The proven system is reinvoked in many parts of the country.

As our Sanskrit quote goes:

* *na coraharyam na ca rajaharyam na*
Bhratrbhajyam na ca bharakari l
Vyaye krte vardhata eva nityam
Vidyadhanam sarvadhvapradhanam

ll

* English translation: "The wealth of knowledge cannot be stolen by thieves, cannot be seized by kings, cannot be divided amongst brothers and is not heavy to carry. The more you spend, the more it grows. It is the most important amongst all kinds of wealth."

Faith of the Kerala Youth: Factors that Promote and Hinder Faith Experience

Thomas J.

How could a man of just thirty years be so powerful? His words continue to inspire many! His actions leave effects even today! The reason was that he realised the power of his youthfulness and channelized it in a proper direction. His 'Abba experience' brought meaning to his life. Youth in our day too are immensely energetic and vibrant. In matters of faith and religion, there is steady growth as well as a decline. This short essay is an effort to look into the factors that attract the youth to Christian faith and also those that prevent them from the faith experience.

The state of Kerala, famous for its Christian tradition, has been imparting the faith experience to many generations down the centuries. One of the major elements in this noble task is family. Catholic families in Kerala are very keen to live

Christian values and impart Christian faith to their children. Parents live as models for their children. They show that it is possible and meaningful to follow Jesus. Parents train their children to attend church everyday or if not possible, every Sunday. They are very particular that they attend catechism classes, whereby they come to know the different dimensions of faith. There is an insistence on family prayer such as Rosary and Bible reading. Many of the priests and religions testify that the inspiration that influenced their vocation is their family atmosphere. The good example of their faithful parents help them overcome hurdles in their life.

The Charismatic Movement that brought a wind of renewal to the Kerala Church from 1970's continues to inspire many youth even today. The increasing number of healing testimonies and conversion attract many young people to join for prayer with them. This movement helps young people to hear the Word of God with enthusiasm and vigour. The counselling they conduct really leaves an imprint on the youth. They are cautioned to put away their meaningless thoughts and look ahead with hope and optimism and find meaning in Christian living. One of my friends from my own parish shared his experience. On a new year's eve, he met with an accident which caused him a leg injury. In a retreat he attended after his medication healed his injury and brought him close to Jesus and the Church. Now he is in the parish council serving the church for its better functioning.

The youth movements such a KCYM (1978) and Jesus Youth (1985) provide ample scope for the youth to come out of themselves and witness to Christian life. It is an aid for them to interact with a peer group that is rooted in Christian faith. The 'full timer program' that the Jesus Youth organises brings the participants in contact with many vibrant mission stations that bravely bear witness to Christian faith amidst life threatening situations. Some have even shared that the experiences have ignited the spark of faith anew in them. A companion of mine who was working in Dubai realised his vocation to priesthood with the continuous assistance of Jesus Youth. Jesus Youth articulates Christian faith in the language and lifestyle of youth that is in a well-accepted movement. The person of Jesus is brought more close to them by the different methods that the group employs.

The Catholic media ventures like 'Goodness TV' and 'Shalom Continue' really make an impact on the youth. The different inspiring programs that they telecast deepen the faith of the youth. Media also works as a platform to express their opinions and views regarding different topics related to faith. There they feel that their opinions are valued and they are accepted. Value oriented programs of these media prevent the youth from misusing media for momentary happiness. It conscientizes them to be on the right track. Media also helps as the unifying force among the youth that they feel connected with many and that they are not just confined to a limited space but rather open to encounter many across the world and enrich themselves by the experience of others.

The other side of the reality is very disappointing. A good number of youth find Christian faith as irrelevant and meaningless. They consider it as an old ideology capable of influencing anyone in the current situation. This shift has

Thomas J.

occurred because of many factors. Liturgy is one of them. The youth today find liturgy dry and lifeless. The rubric oriented liturgy is dead for them. The translation of the new Malayalam missal has won much criticism in this regard. Instead of full and lively participation of all the faithful, it distances them from the mysteries that they are celebrating. The youth wants to celebrate liturgy with full vigour, but in reality they find monotony. Because of this drawback they are attracted to evil practices like Black Mass and Satan worship.

Other hindrance for them is the prejudice of the elect. Some priests and elders in the parishes think that the youth do not have spiritual depth and so cannot contribute anything to the church. As such, they maintain a gap between them. This most often turns to be a wide gap. They are neither given a say in parochial matters nor are they encouraged to come to the mainstream. Many youth have shared with me the unreasonable humiliation they have suffered from their own spiritual leaders. The 'Divide and Rule' policy of some of the administrators affects the youth very badly. They lose their friendship and win enemies. Because of this attitude of the administration they look at faith and church as fraud. They find alternatives in political ideologies and movements that do not promote life. This is a dangerous situation.

The lack of role models is another hindrance. Youth always look for someone whom they can imitate. They look for a channel to Jesus and are the most often disappointed. The news about the immoral life of the church authority really puzzles young minds. Because of the spiritual interest of the media, the youth tend to generalise particular events. They look at the church for spiritual leadership and find mere administration. The church for its survival sometimes counter witnesses its values. This causes a decline in the faith of the youth. So they tend to adapt to leaders which momentarily advocate momentary happiness and gain.

Another factor that hinders them is that their questions go unanswered, their doubts remain unclarified. They find no competent personnel who can answer their challenging queries and enlighten them with new insights. The homilies and reflections they find monotonous, shallow and dogmatic. So it does not inspire them. Those who have monopoly over religions truth are reluctant to manifest them in the language of the youth.

As these two tendencies of pro and against faith grow together in Kerala youth, it is high time to promote the positive side and improve upon the negative. We need to find alternatives through which Jesus can be shown as relevant for them today. The youth need a God-experience and for that energetic movements must be given space in the church. The church leadership is challenged by the youth to concentrate on the spirituality rather than the administration.

Let's give space for the youth, otherwise the church will lose its vigour. Let them realise and channelize the power of their youthfulness for a better tomorrow.

Thomas J.

Feeling the Freedom

Tinu S. Augustine

A big question arises after hearing the word 'freedom'. Today we are fed up with lots of options. But, do we have real freedom of choice? The world is full of 'free' entities. It rules markets, families, business, education and even communication. These 'frees' come with a footnote of conditions to be applied. Freedom is not rightly expressed in those 'freebies'. Humans are born free, but they are in chains everywhere. Freedom at its various realms needs proper definition. Freedom of expression needs further clarifications. Today, a lot of discussions are going on regarding the right of expressions. This applies to many aspects like religious freedom, social freedom, freedom of expression in art and literature, especially in visual media and films.

Freedom of expression is as important and as fundamental as the freedom of life. The Indian Constitution guarantees this in the 19th article. Thus, it has a constitutional privilege to be ensured and protected by law. This freedom is never to be curtailed by anybody who is under this law. The right of expression at its root is the basic way of demanding one's necessities and conveying one's thoughts to somebody else. When it attains bigger meanings, it becomes the expression of one's faith, creativity, criticism and strategies. It also projects one's inner feelings, emotions, from the depths to the outer world. So, the genuineness of this has to be maintained without any addition or deletion. If and only if a person is free to express what he/she thinks it gets the status of a right.

Who has the right to censor one's creativity? The greatest threat to freedom of expression is censorship. The act of cutting down one's right to express is called censoring. It is done directly and lawfully in the field of films. Because the government appointed censor board functions with this motive. In the case of literature, public speeches, use of social media and religious rights of expression, there is another strategy. Some high powers indirectly control or restrict the freedom here. It happens often when criticisms are raised against a political party, politician, a group or an institution. There can be cases of extreme criticisms. But even small scale threats are spotted and weeded out in the beginning itself. This becomes the denial of the fundamental right to expression. Once again the question resonates, "who has the right to limit the right of expression?"

The present Indian scenario suggests a redefining of the right to express oneself. There are some occasions where we are compelled to limit our freedom. There are also some situations which demand to have some particular expressions as well. During the last year, India faced some issues regarding the screening of the national anthem in the theatres before films. There were also some problems of suppressing certain

Tinu S. Augustine

authors like Taslima Nasreen of Bangla Desh, and Kalburgi in Karnataka. The murder of the journalist Gauri Lankesh is the last nail on the coffin. Another major hindrance in this field is the national censor board. It cuts and shortens scenes and dialogues of films after the director's cut. In the realm of religion, intolerance emerges as part of a growing sense of nationalism. Social level sufferings emerge in the form of demonetization and unique identification policies.

The youth respond quickly. Technology and wide networks of communication add to it. Any kind of protest or a new stream of thought attains widespread attention in no time. In the cases of Delhi gang rape, Jisha murder in Kerala and many similar instances, social media played a major role in firing up public attention. People use media as a tool to express their different views or responses on public issues. Already defined in the Constitution, criticism can be made on anything and anybody except some reverential positions like the President and the Supreme Court. In democracy this type of criticism is often required as part of building up of the nation in an integrated manner. It was the famous cartoonist and novelist O.V. Vijayam who wrote 'Dharma Purana' against the period of emergency in 1975. As satirical as it was, no action was taken against it.

Freedom always brings responsibility. It comes from inside. One should be responsible to oneself while exercising one's freedom to express. At the same time it is not to be imposed. Freedom of expression follows from human freedom, but human freedom presupposes natural moral law of human will and intellect. Freedom of expression applies to the freedom in art, literature, films, politics, society, customs and religion. Moral choice is as important as the freedom of choice. Before blaming others for curtailing one's ideas, one must cross examine oneself. This requires a sense of the society, knowing the pulse of the people who receive the products of our expression. It demands prudence, wisdom and integrity of the one who expresses oneself. It is unfair to defame any person through words or actions. This fundamental right to express ourselves is never to be thought of as a means to fulfil the revenge on somebody. This is where at least some media often fail today.

As the fourth estate, the media is always powerful. The choice of what to express is called media ethics. The media has the power to stabilize or sterilize a government. It has control over the thinking pattern of people. It creates history. It manipulates truth. It educates. It brainwashes. A high moral is, thus, essential in expressing our opinions. Freedom is not something that destroys. Freedom creates. God created the world with divine free will. Creation is thus an expression of God's love out of divine freedom. Human freedom has thus a divine dimension. Freedom of expression is to tend towards self realization. It ultimately leads to the realization of the divine. It is the mystical union with God. Pope Francis calls this expression as the 'Joy of the Gospel'. There lies the ultimate aim of any kind of expression. It should be followed with joy of the hearts of one who expresses and the one who receives it.

Freedom is to be freed. It is true that there can be some limitations for our freedom of expression. But it should not be from some vested interests. Tolerance is a deciding factor. Openness is another. Modernism emerged as a criticism of

Tinu S. Augustine

the scholastic medieval period. But in fact, it was because the church opened her doors towards arts, literature and science. She accepted criticism positively ever since that reformation. The Hegelian dialectics develops in such an environment. Any thesis can have an antithesis in order to be synthesized. It requires freedom. Suppression does no good to progress. It ignites revolt. Being a good listener is the first stage of openness. Wisdom monitors thereafter.

Importance of Tolerance
Xavier Thomas

What is the most resilient parasite? An idea. Resilient. Highly contagious. Once an idea has taken hold of the brain, it's almost impossible to eradicate it. That's the power of an idea. It persuades a person to fulfil something, right and wrong. For any individual, one's personal idea always seems to be relevant, whether or not one bothers about whether it's right and wrong, unless one spends much time thinking about that idea. Usually, it's the lack of rational thinking that makes a person judgemental and mistakenly believe certain prejudiced ideas to be true. Consequently, we fall into the trap of intolerance.

Intolerance is the unwillingness to accept views, beliefs, or behaviour that differs from one's own. The quality or state of being intolerant can also mean exceptional sensitivity (Webster). What makes this phenomenon threatening is that people simply do not accept ideas that are at variance to their own ideas, especially those that contrast and are in conflict with the concepts that they had moulded in their minds from their young ages. This is what makes them hostile. Consequences of this behaviour are that people tend to destroy those who threaten their ideas and beliefs, even though these others are right.

"Our explanation of present-past rapport removes man from the strict determinism according to which psychic life is determined by prior causes rather than by rational will." (A. Cencini and A. Manenti, 331). Intolerance, rationally, is one of the hot topics today. News about the occurrence of intolerance is reported in certain regions. But, are we sure that it only occurs in those places which are acknowledged or reported by newsrooms? No, it isn't. It is happening, everyday, and that's the truth.

In "Psychology and Formation", A. Cencini and A. Manenti claim that, "Total freedom is never accessible to man. His partial freedom too, is never a given fact, but a conquest. Human beings are not born free, but become free. Being born free is a literary concept, not psychological. To begin with, man is in a condition of determinism, and in the measure in which he succeeds to come out of it, he will become the creator of himself." And they continue saying that, "It has become a symbol of his existence, or at least of that sort of existence which means a lot because it is created by him. This area of greater or lesser freedom is what we have called the 'second dimension', the most suitable area for educative action."

Searching intolerance inside ourselves is much easier than finding it outside. For example, family is considered as one of the serious institutions of society. It's the family that makes and moulds who we are today. Family is like a foundation-stone to building society. This means that the family's role is unavoidable for the existence of society,

The family is the nursery where we are told to learn values, virtues, morals, habits and principles. All these are given to us only because the parents care that much and want their kids to mingle with others or adjust with society so that everything would fall in place. Here, the wishes of the kids are ignored and they are forced to do certain things. Still, technically, it is intolerance.

In "The Art of Expecting", Veronique Vienne says that, "Children will always respect you if you tell them the truth. When they question the reason why you want them to behave a certain way, don't try to bribe them, threaten them, or deceive them" (76). She continues saying that, "Let's say you insist your baby must go to sleep at a certain time, worried as you are that if you don't put him on a schedule, you'll attract the wrath of every childcare expert in the Western or Eastern hemisphere. What happens, sure enough, is that your infant boy makes a point of never nodding off before midnight" (71).

This viewpoint comes from a caring parent who desires that his/her child should have a healthy sleep. Maybe the child wants to spend some time with its' parents, but knowingly or unknowingly, the parent is forcing the kid to do something that the kid doesn't want to do even though it is not considered as something threatening. My argument is that a person can do so unknowingly. That's what human nature is, which follows a predetermined pattern, like a parent.

"Man must do good if he wants to live well", "Man must eat if he wants to live well." These are two totally different expressions (A. Cencini and A. Manenti, 112).

A child may want to become an artist or an art student but its' parents may persuade it to study provisional courses, believing that the kid would have a brighter future if it does so. The parents, intentionally or unintentionally, are forcing their own interests onto their kids and try to support their argument by claiming that "it will only do good for you." Note that in many households, when a boy is born, the parents want him to become a police officer or an engineer. If it's a girl, she should be a doctor or a teacher. Here, parents are instilling their own ideas or wishes to their kids, instead of understanding what might be the unique capacity or strength of their kids.

The practice of dowry is prohibited, legally, but it is still practised in our society today. Not every bride's family is interested or even capable of giving dowry. Yet, for them, maybe giving dowry is all about giving a secure married life to their girls. In a way, this phenomenon too is intolerant in nature, for it is like forcing the other to pay so that we can give young women a secured peaceful life.

Gender discrimination too is active in families. For example, wanting a boy child instead of a girl is a common wish for most parents. That's why the rate of female foeticide is higher in some areas, especially in the northern states of India. It should also be noted that honour killings are still active. Girls who elope with the boys they love are slaughtered by their parents in the name of protecting their status. It is shocking to know that such killings are considered to be sacred in their regions.

Strangely, has anyone heard about a boy killed by his parents to keep the status of the family?

Intolerance has probably played a great role in the origin of nuclear families beginning with anything, from having difference of opinions to having different behaviours. Or, it could even be the result of quarrels between a daughter-in-law and her mother-in-law or also certain disagreement in taking some decisions among family members. These are some of the factors that gave birth to the nuclear family.

Intolerance is also seen in love relationships. Not every family supports their child to enter into a love relationship with a person from another caste or religion without their consent. This cannot be judged either as positive or negative since, for some families it's about choosing the right ones for their kids. However, for others, it's about avoiding a bad name or keeping up the good status of their family.

"The efforts of men to obtain greater acceptance of their own values and patterns of living do result in a greater regularity and predictability of social behaviour. The assumption, however, that men in general are concerned with the advantages of regularity or predictability of conduct is difficult to accept without also assuming that the average man possesses a high degree of insight and social understanding." (Roucek, 7). The issue of reservations is another controversial one; for, even the protesters of reservation would use their status to get admissions in educational institutions. When it comes to education, there always would be a disciplinary boundary, especially in private firms. There, they follow a clichéd pattern that "everyone should follow rules and it's for the greater good and will give your kids a bright future." Instantly, almost every parent will approach those firms without any doubt, believing that they are doing right. Strict rules make kids unable to speak or utter a word, making them to learn more by pressuring more. Absolutely there's competition between private institutions and it's all about having or achieving good grades. The question is, are we really making a good tomorrow for the kids?

"Ordinarily one's first reaction to the term 'religion' is to think of the powers ascribed to gods or other supernatural beings and man's relations or other supernatural powers and his actions in obtaining their favour or avoiding their hostility, and the influence of these recognised relations upon the control of man's behaviour as an individual or as a member of a group." (Roucek, 101).

The term 'education' can't be limited to one meaning, because it is subject to many interpretations. It's an expansive term. According to the Merriam Webster dictionary, education is "the process of receiving or giving systematic instructions, especially at a school or a university", "a body of knowledge acquired while being educated" and "information about or training in a particular subject." They are not the only meanings; it signifies a process as long as human experiences grow. Education is not only something that happens academically; it is also something that an individual absorbs from his/her daily life. Possibly, it begins in the mother's womb. As Brown and Roucek state, education is "the sum total of the experience which moulds the attitudes and determines the conduct of both the child and the adult" (Roucek, 131).

The reason we are talking about intolerance is because we are educated to think about different perspectives. The question is, isn't there any intolerance in educational institutions too?

"The schools should confine themselves, it is said, to teaching practically useful skills and knowledge. Such argument is sometimes convenient when educational costs are under consideration" (Roucek, 131).

It is sad that primitive dogmas and unjust structures like the 'varna system' are still active today. The very idea has been embedded like a foundation stone in our minds. For example, people will cheer you when you help an old woman to cross the road. Does that happen if you help a beggar to cross the road? Maybe, helping a beggar to cross the road is going to be partly imagination, but the applauding part might transform to blaming. Because, willingly or unwillingly, 'varna' system is deeply rooted, and people surely will judge others with that perspective.

What religion truly teaches is peace and harmony, but the ideas are then misinterpreted by some for personal benefit, and that results into chaos. The birth of communal riots begins with these interpretations.

Intolerance is also active in the current newsrooms which have a remarkable influence in our lives. But they are in the business of selling news. Finding facts isn't always their top priority. They still instil an idea into the reader or audience. What happens if they publish fake news? Of course the readers will believe it, not everyone though. At least not for a long time. That's where I'm trying to shed some light. Selling news without any genuine evidence to increase circulation and ratings is intolerant in nature. Newsrooms need to be trustworthy in order to inspire and influence the formation or development of our own perception. If truth is told by all, the world would change.

Can intolerance be good at certain times or is it always negative as the word suggests? If some intolerance can be considered positive, what could be the dividing line between positive and negative intolerance? On an ethical level, what is tolerance and what is intolerance? How can one define the border dividing tolerance and intolerance? Or is the whole idea a matter of different perspectives; where perspectives may be defined by the direct result of first hand social experiences?

References

A Cencini and A. Manenti, *Psychology and Formation*, Bologna, S.E Paul Publications, 1985.

Joseph S. Roucek, *Social Control*, New York, D. Van Nostrand Company, 1956.

Veronique Vienne, *The Art of Expecting*, New York, Clarkson Potter, 2002.

Contributors

Ajith C. is pursuing Theological studies under the Trichur Archdiocese, Kerala.

Aloysius T. Antony completed M.A. Sociology from Loyola College of Social Sciences, Trivandrum. Now pursuing Theological studies.

Amal Tom George is a media professional and communicator. He works with teenagers to keep them away from substance abuse.

Amardeep is a Jesuit scholastic and a student of English Literature at St. Joseph's College Devagiri, Calicut.

Angela Jinny is pursuing Masters in English Literature from Saint Berchmans College Changanassery, Kerala.

Anju Rose is pursuing higher studies in Kerala.

Anju Teresa did her post graduation in English Language and Literature. She was the former Guest Lecturer in the Department of English, Pavanatma College, Murickassery, Idukki and she also worked at Alphonsa College Pala.

Aparana Thomas pursuing Masters in English Language and Literature from Vimala College (Autonomous) Thrissur.

Ashly Paul an English Literature student from St. Xavier's College, Aluva, Kerala. Currently pursuing Masters in English Literature from Central University of Kerala.

Ashmi Mary Mathew is a graduate in English Literature.

Cerin Babu works as an Assistant Professor in the Department of English at Vimala College, Thrissur.

Jess George is pursuing higher studies in Kerala.

Joyal Jose Panachipuram CST from the Little Flower Congregation, at present pursuing Masters in English Literature.

Karunyamaria a Carmelite nun pursuing her P. hd. in English Literature in Changanassery, Kerala.

Linda Therese Luiz Assistant Professor, Department of Sociology, St. Teresa's College Ernakulam. Teaching at St. Teresa's College for the past four years.

Maria Sharol is pursuing Master's in English Literature from Alphonsa College, Pala.

Naveen Joemon is in priesthood formation for the Changanachery Archdiocese, Kerala.

Naveen Thomas an English literature student from Newman College, Thodupuzha. A gentle soul who believes in pouring out head through letters and ink. Passionate though not perfect.

Neenu Jose completed B.Sc. and M.Sc. Mathematics from Newman College Thodupuzha. A passionate human who tries to provide insight into reality beyond imagination and emotions beyond feelings.

Rachel Berkumon is pursuing her BA English from Sacred Heart College, Thevara, Kochi. She loves reading books, especially English fiction.

Santhwana belongs to the Congregation of Daughters of Mary. She will be completing 25 years in religious life. She is a Physics teacher in Trivandrum.

Steffi Rose Babu is pursuing higher studies in Kerala.

Tarun Eldo Mathew a college dropout fighting physical illness. Loves to read extensively and watch movies and co-owns a resto-café in his hometown. Pursuing an acting career which goes in hand with his love for drama and theatre.

Thomas J. pursuing Theology at Carmelgiri Alwaye after completing philosophical studies at JDV, Pune.

Tinu S. Augustine is pursuing Theology in Vadavathoor Seminary Kottayam and aspiring to become a holy and zealous priest.

Xavier Thomas completed M.A English Literature from Deva Matha College, Kuravilangad. He reads and writes, aware of how words and books are magic for the parched souls. As paint is to an artist, words are to him for he has known their power in preserving and destroying.

www.ingramcontent.com/pod-product-compliance
Lightning Source LLC
Chambersburg PA
CBHW031311280626
47169CB00018B/1238